THE END OF
THE MILDEW GANG

THE END OF
THE MILDEW GANG

Being the Third Volume
In the Mildew Gang Trilogy

AN INSPECTOR CAULDRON
CLASSIC CRIME NOVEL

by

S. FOWLER WRIGHT

WRITING AS "SYDNEY FOWLER"

The Borgo Press
An Imprint of Wildside Press LLC

MMVIII

CONTENTS

CHAPTER I.

Inspector Cauldron Cannot Refuse

CORNELIUS MILDEW was dead, but Inspector Cauldron, considering a murder which, however criminal in itself, was satisfactory to the police, saw no reason to hope that there would be a consequent end of the Mildew Gang. Had he died, as he had surely deserved, at the end of a noosed rope, and by due process of law, it would have been a far different matter; but Mr. Mildew had come to his violent end in undiminished reputation of wealthy and benevolent respectability.

His connection with the ruthless international gang of drug traffickers from which the bulk of his huge income had been derived remained a police presumption which the inquest did not disclose. The verdict had been that he had died, during the temporary insanity of convention, by a shot from his own hand. So the public record would be; but Inspector Cauldron saw reason for a different opinion. He said confidently, in the official privacy of Superintendent Backwash's room, that the finger of the Hon. Peter Boyle had pulled the trigger, aiming thereby both to avert the disclosures which would have followed the arrest of the murdered man, and himself secure control of the Mildew Gang.

He had acted thus in a confident belief that the police had no knowledge of his connection with its illicit traffic, and that he had only to leave the scene of the crime unnoticed for no suspicion to be directed upon him.

On these last points he was wrong, and it was an error in which he would remain, if Inspector Cauldron could have his way. "It's the one good card in a pack from which we've lost most of the trumps now that Mildew's dead," he said, with as much optimism as the position allowed; and Superintendent Backwash, who had been discussing the case with the Assistant Commissioner at an earlier hour, replied: "Well, it's to be left in your hands. I've arranged that."

Inspector Cauldron looked gratified. To a young officer, and one who was aware that his college background was a barrier of distance, if not of hostility, between him and some of his superior officers who were of a different tradition, it was an opportunity such as many years of service might not have won. He knew that it was merit, not favour, which had been rewarded with this assignment; that it marked his superiors' approval of his conduct of that which had already come to his hands by its chance connection with a different, more ordinary crime, and even that investigation, but for the sudden illness of a more experienced officer, would not have been left to him. Yet even so, merit does not always find the recognition that it deserves. He knew that Superintendent Backwash had been his friend. He said: "Thanks. And I shall have Miss Wingrove with me, of course?"

He saw the look of hesitation on the superintendent's face, and added hastily: "We promised her that." And then, in a changed voice, as a doubt of what that hesitation could mean entered his mind: "She's not backing out, is she?"

"Not that I've heard. The question is whether we didn't promise too much. There's the fact that they know her already, and, if you put her on to it you may rouse the suspicion you wish particularly to avoid."

"We should have to be careful about that, but it might be an advantage in other ways."

"Pigs might fly. I'll tell you this. Tolbooth's dead against our letting her have anything further to do with the case. Said we shall be mugs if we do.... And there's her safety to consider as well.

"It comes to this. I know we promised her, and if she holds us to it we don't want to refuse. But from now on you'll be in charge of the case. If you ask for Miss Wingrove's help, we'll assign her to you. But it will be your responsibility. If anything goes wrong, you've been warned, and you'll get the blame."

"That's a safe guess; though it doesn't sound fair to me. But, if you put it like that, you know I've got to have her. She's got our word for it, and I couldn't get out of it if I tried."

"No," the superintendent replied dryly. "I don't say you could." He added: "If you're asked to send in your resignations there's no law against getting married afterwards. Not if you're both alive."

Inspector Cauldron flushed angrily. "I don't know why on earth you should say that. I've never—and I don't suppose such an idea's ever entered her head. Why, till after she'd gone off to Scotland, we all thought she was engaged to Limbrook."

"Except Tolbooth. Still, you're the best judge. I always thought she was an extremely sensible girl.

Inspector Cauldron looked better pleased as he heard this, thinking that it had a complimentary sound, but he thought again and was less sure.

CHAPTER II.

Miss Wingrove Requires a Husband

BILLIE WINGROVE came out of Staccato's and took a taxi to the headquarters of the C.I.D., where Inspector Cauldron was waiting for her report.

"Yes, I've seen him," she said. "I should know him anywhere now. It isn't a face you'd forget quickly."

"He didn't notice you?"

"No. Why should he? I only stood in the doorway for a moment. There were people going in and out all the time."

"You're sure you'd never seen him before?"

"Certain. I don't see how or where he should have seen me. It's not likely at all."

"No. I don't think it is. It might have been worth while, as you were there, to get near him, and see what you could overhear."

"I couldn't have done that. Not in these clothes."

"I don't see—"

"No. You wouldn't.... But," she added more kindly, seeing the hurt expression on the inspector's face which her retorts too frequently produced, "you're quite bright in some ways.... You say he often has the same table?"

"Yes. Sometimes with lady friends. Sometimes alone."

"There were two with him tonight."

"Yes. The Misses Midhurst. We're checking up on all his friends. But there's no harm in them. Rich and dull. We might manage to get someone to introduce you to them under another name, and you'd get to know him through them."

"He's often with them?"

"Yes. Just at present. Wants to make some use of them, of course."

"They look decent."

"So they probably are."

10

"Well, that would be one way. But I've thought of something quicker. Could you get me a respectable husband by this time to-morrow?"

"If you mean this for a proposal—"

"Don't be silly. He'd know you more likely than not. I want someone I've never met. Someone who'll look as though he might dine there regularly, and take his...."

"Any other qualifications?"

"Yes. He'll have to be the sort of man who'll leave the table on sudden business—not the first night—without remembering to come back, or that I haven't money to pay the bill."

"It might succeed." The tone was more doubtful than the words. Inspector Cauldron had to remind himself that the obligations of his office were more important than the pleasure of acting husband to a girl he liked, or the possible danger of what she proposed to do.

"There's no reason it shouldn't," she answered confidently. "Unless you can think of a better plan."

But as Inspector Cauldron had no better one to propose, he could only say: "You'll have to sheer off at the first sign of recognition, however slight, or even if you think there's a doubt in his mind. If he started enquiring, he'd be sure to find out who you are, and he'd stick at nothing to—"

"Of course. I see that. If he didn't trust me, there'd be no sense in going on. I should be no use at all."

"I don't think the worst danger's with him. It's that he may introduce you to someone of the gang that you've met before."

"Or they may see us together. That's why we shall have to work fast. But the first thing is for you to get me the best husband you can."

Inspector Cauldron did not doubt that this detail could be arranged, but he felt that it required the assistance of higher powers. He went to consult Superintendent Backwash, and met Chief Inspector Tolbooth leaving that gentleman's office.

"How's it going?" he asked with a friendliness which was more sparingly shown to those of equal rank to his own; and, when he heard what was proposed, he gave it a benediction which Inspector Cauldron was glad to have.

"It's a thousand to one," he said, "that he won't recognize a girl that it's a hundred to one that he's never seen. He'll have heard all about her, of course; but that's different. And a married woman, and differently dressed, and he not thinking we're on his track at all.... No, it's a safe bet, if she does it properly, he'll suspect nothing at all; and you can trust her for that. It's not often you get looks and

11

brains under one hat, but—why don't you get someone to marry her in earnest? It oughtn't to be a hard job, and there'd be no need to have the ring charged to our expenses account."

Inspector Cauldron said irritably: "Of course, she wouldn't do anything of the kind."

"No? How do you know she hasn't got someone in mind for the part? That may be what gave her the idea?"

"Because, if she had, she wouldn't have asked me to find him."

"How do you know she won't turn him down, and bring out her own exhibit...? But," he added, more seriously, "I'll tell you one thing, Boyle isn't likely to have any of his gang at Staccato's, or hanging anywhere round there. He's far too wary for that. If Miss Wingrove only meets him there, I should say there's very little risk that she'll see anyone she'd rather not. It would be another matter if she went about with him in other places. She'd have to be very cautious of that."

"Then the next thing seems to be to get hold of the right man."

* * * * * * *

Mr. Albert Risdon's blue saloon car halted at the pavement, and Billie Wingrove, coming out of the side exit of the London Pavilion with commendable punctuality, got in, and sat down at her husband's side. She had no need to identify the car with a second glance, for she had its number, which was beyond duplication.

Inspector Cauldron, watching inconspicuously from the opposite corner, felt that the occasion for jealousy should not arise. To him, the man whom Superintendent Backwash had chosen was of an appearance that no sensible woman would approve. He decided that he lacked charm. Yet such men do continue their species, which implies wives.

But Mr. Risdon had another quality, more important in the superintendent's eyes than any presence or lack of charm. He lacked curiosity. And what was required of him was of a simplicity which could not easily err, especially as he did not know the full purpose of what he did.

He could not make the mistake of using Billie's real name, which he did not know. His wife was to be Clara to him. He could, on the reliable authority of the friend of Superintendent Backwash who had brought him upon the scene, be trusted to treat her in the casual manner of an established husband, for he treated all women thus.

Billie looked at her pseudo spouse with friendly but appraising eyes. His own were on the road, as they ought to be. He said: "I suppose we go straight there?"

"Yes," he said, "it's about the right time—Albert. Or should I say Bert?"

"It's a free country," he said, giving her a half glance which showed little consciousness of the attractions of the wife who had been so curiously thrust upon him. "Most people do."

"Then it must be right for your wife.... Or doesn't she...? Or am I the only one?"

"I'm not married, if you mean that."

"I expect that makes it a bit simpler. But I don't suppose you'll have me on your hands for more than a few nights—evenings I should have said."

Billie became aware with a furious inward anger that she was blushing at the implication of an ill-chosen word. Surely she was not such a...? But a well-started blush is beyond control.

However, Albert appeared unconscious alike of her confusion or any occasion for it. He answered with more politeness in the words than the casual tone in which they were said: "If it's dozens, I shan't mind."

"Well, it wouldn't be as bad as though we were what we pretend. I mean, you won't have to go on paying for me. I suppose the police will be doing that."

"You bet. I shouldn't have been likely to take it on else."

Obviously not. But Billie considered that it might have been better put. She would have agreed with Inspector Cauldron that Albert lacked charm. She said: "Here we are.... Yes, but I wasn't sure that you'd know the place.... You'd better let me go first. I know where I want us to sit."

"You'll have to wait in the vestibule a few minutes while I get rid of the car."

"Very well."

The dining-room at Staccato's opens directly into the outer hall. Seated there, Billie could see the corner which the Hon. Peter Boyle frequented, and was almost sure that he had not come. That was well, for, if they were in their seats first, there could be no appearance of deliberately getting near him.

Joined by Bert, she led the way directly to the table where she had seen him before, and the head waiter, observing strangers to enter where most of the customers were known, steered his course as directly to her.

Offering to seat herself at Boyle's table, she expected to be guided to one of those nearby, which, at this early hour, were equally vacant, but the head waiter made no demur, placing her chair with the bland obsequiousness natural to his kind.

This seemed even better than she could have reasonably expected. Was she to have the Hon. Peter at her right hand for the many opportunities which a dinner gives? No, she found, she was not, for this evening at least, for the gentleman did not come. And when she rose at last from a prolonged meal, and asked that the seats they had occupied should be reserved for the next night, she was told, with polite regret, that it was impossible, as the table was already engaged. Very well, she said, the next one would do. The name? Mr. and Mrs. Risdon. The waiter wrote it down. She could depend upon the seats being reserved

She left with some depression, feeling that the evening had been wasted, but Superintendent Backwash thought differently.

"You've made a good start," he said, "that isn't likely to rouse suspicion. You never know with these gangs. Even one of the waiters there may be in it. Boyle might use him to pass notes to those who would go there at different times. Now, tomorrow you'd better go early. Be sure to get there before Boyle, and come away as soon as your meal's done. Don't linger or take the slightest notice of him. It'll be the surest way in the end."

Billie recognized the voice of experience, and that there was wisdom in what it said. She went early on the next night, and was already well advanced upon the entrée course before the Hon. Peter sat down, this time with two male companions, at the adjoining table.

The men with whom he came were strangers to her. Fragments of conversation which reached her ears were of a political rather than a business character, and certainly, unless they talked in code, which she was disinclined to believe, were not concerned with illicit traffic of any kind

Her attention to the next table, which, for this occasion, must be of ears rather than eyes, was rendered easier by the fact that Albert Risdon talked little, his mind being primarily fixed upon what he ate. Yet he talked at times, with an indifference to what went on around him which she must endeavour to equal.

She found occasion to look closely at Peter Boyle, without attracting his attention. She tried to read what he was, in a woman's way, which it was surely important for her to know.

She saw a man who was still young, with straw-coloured, short-cropped hair, slightly but not flabbily rotund, with a rather round though otherwise hard-featured face, quietly though expensively dressed—a gentleman by conventional standards, superficially pleasant in manner, and very confident of himself. He was not one whom, had she met him in other ways, would have appeared to her to be of a criminal type, but now she heard a hard note in the pleasant voice, and read cruelty in firm, rather thin lips.

She noticed also that he was exacting in what he ate, twice sending back plates which were not to his precise requirement. Doubtless he paid freely, but he would have value for what he paid. He attached importance to physical comfort; and to such a man, his own fortune being precarious, the opportunity to acquire wealth, by whatever means, would be hard to resist.

The fragments of conversation she caught appeared to relate to the position of a parliamentary under-secretary, who might be called upon to resign, which one of Boyle's companions was being persuaded by the other two to use his influence to avert. There might be some connection between that and the activities of the Mildew Gang, but it seemed unlikely to her. Anyway, she did not delay after her companion's meal came to its somewhat protracted conclusion. "I think we ought to be going now, Bert," she said, with a faint asperity in her voice which carried to the next table, and drew the attention of the Hon. Peter, so that their eyes met as she rose, and she was conscious that his remained upon her after her own had turned indifferently away.

CHAPTER III.

A Young Wife in Trouble

MR. AND MRS. RISDON went to Staccato's every night during the next week, twice again seeing Boyle there with different friends, and then, on the next occasion, Billie decided that it was time to try the trick for which such-elaborate preparations had been made. So she told her partner as they drove through Piccadilly, and made one or two final suggestions as to the details of the event, which were rather brusquely received.

"Yes," he said impatiently, "Superintendent Backwash explained all that."

"It's just as well in these matters to leave nothing to chance, she retorted, with a sharpness which did not come into her voice for the first time in dealing with this adopted husband, who, in the short period of their association, she had come near to actively disliking. Not that he took any unfair advantage of his position. Rather the other way! Of course, it would have been intolerable if he had; but still there might be some awareness of opportunity. Of course, an oversensitive honour—but no, she could not delude herself in that way. And now she began to doubt whether Superintendent Backwash might not have made an absolute error in his selection. Would Risdon be equal to doing even the short and simple part which was required of him in a natural manner?

Actually, he was not; but, all the same, the superintendent's astuteness was not condemned.

Peter Boyle arrived almost as soon as themselves. He had with him the Misses Midhurst, whom Billie had seen on her first visit to the restaurant. A nearer inspection approved Inspector Cauldron's description of them. If she were any judge of her sex, there were no criminal secrets contained in their bovine heads. She observed, without a direct glance, as most women can, that their dresses were costly in material rather than design, that they wore valuable but old-fashioned jewellery, and that their podgy figures were such as will make the most skilful dressmaker despair.

She saw also that they were animated beyond what she supposed to be their normal conditions. "I don't suppose," she thought unkindly, "that they could be roused to greater excitement by anything less than a bomb." Two minutes later she had concluded that Peter Boyle was paying serious court to the younger woman, who was obviously flattered by his attentions. What could be the meaning of that? Natural attraction? It was scarcely a possible explanation. Money? He was getting plenty in his own nefarious manner. There must be some other motive, which it might be worth her while to discover. She began to doubt whether she would not do better to abandon her purpose for this occasion, and concentrate on hearing what she could; and while she hesitated, considering what discreet words she could choose to convey her meaning to one who was not always quick to understand an oblique phrase, her chance went, for Albert brought his hand down on the table with a bang that rattled silver and glass, and drew the attention of those around as he exclaimed: "Hang it all! There's a man I've got to meet at the club, and I clean forgot." He pulled out his watch and stared at it with a scared expression. "I'll have to bolt, Clara," he said loudly; "it may mean hundreds to me." He picked up his hat, which he had made a habit of depositing against the rail of his chair, pushed awkwardly past an astonished waiter, and hurried out through the swing-doors, with his eyes fixed on the ground.

It was a performance which had been carefully rehearsed in his own mind, and which he thought he had done well. So he had. Much better than he was likely to guess.

The eyes of the head-waiter, hovering near, met those of Peter Boyle, and the eyebrows of that gentleman lifted slightly. As clearly as though they exchanged words, they had agreed that it was a false performance, very clumsily done. Peter Boyle's eyes were directed upon the abandoned wife, and his conclusion was strengthened by signs of anger and confusion which she was not instant to hide.

Her thought was: "He's ruined everything I never thought he'd be such a fool as that. Why couldn't he do it in a quiet, natural way?" And then, being far from a fool herself, she saw that it was a folly that might be no hindrance to her.

She was confirmed in this opinion as she heard the waiter's voice at her side, deferential but firm: "Madam would like her bill?"

It was an insult, however civilly spoken, for she had not finished a normal meal, and she saw that, if the Hon. Peter should fail to play his allotted part, there might be some real unpleasantness to

be faced, though she might have no fear of ultimate legal consequences, being assured of the powerful protection of Scotland Yard.

"The bill?" she echoed, with an agitation not entirely assumed,
and all the more natural in consequence. "Yes, of course. But I haven't finished yet. At least—yes, of course."

She opened her handbag as she spoke, and drew out a notecase
the emptiness of which was apparent to a dozen pairs of surrounding
eyes, at which she made an effort to look surprised.

"I'm afraid," she said, "I haven't got that much with me. Mr.
Risdon left so hurriedly, I'm sure he didn't think.... I suppose it will
be alright if he pays you tomorrow. You won't mind waiting till
then?'

By this time she had so far forgotten the purpose of what she
did that she felt a real desire to obtain the consent which would have
wrecked the plan so elaborately prepared. But the head-waiter was
now at the side of his subordinate, and took control of the conversation.

"Madam's husband will be sure to return when he recalls that
he left her with the bill unpaid."

"I don't think," she replied, with some recovery of her wits and
her self-control, "that we can be sure of that. He's so forgetful. And
he wouldn't know that I was so short."

"Then perhaps Madam would like to telephone to the gentleman's club?"

"I'm afraid that I don't know what club it is."

The head-waiter's incredulity showed through the veneer of his
habitual deference—a veneer which was wearing thin. "Perhaps
Madam will be kind enough to come with me to the office?"

The polite words were an order not to be disobeyed. There was
as much of genuine as simulated appeal in Billie's eyes as she
turned them directly toward the Hon. Peter. There was no doubt that
his eyes would be upon her. Everyone's were.

She met a glance which was hard to read. The Hon. Peter had
learnt the importance of keeping his thoughts unbetrayed by facial
expression. But she judged correctly that she had failed. He appeared gravely interested, but wholly aloof. Well, it must be the
manager's office for her, and the best get-out she could contrive!
After all, she thought with sudden relief, as she *had* failed, a call to
Inspector Cauldron on the manager's telephone would end any further fuss over the bill. But it would not be pleasant to admit the failure of her elaborate and rather expensive trap....

It was Boyle's younger companion who interrupted this moment's thought. She was fumbling in her bag, and saying: "If I could

be of any assistance—if you would excuse—" Billie saw that she was apologizing nervously for what she offered to do. "She's a dear," she thought, with an instant's regret of her previous contemptuous judgement; "but it's failure for me, just the same...." And then she saw it was not.

For the Hon Peter had been roused to action. "No, Bella," he was saying, in his pleasantest voice, "you'd better leave this to me." His own notecase was out. He turned to Billie to say: "Of course, we saw how it was. It's a thing that might happen to any of us. If you'll be kind enough to allow me—" He held out two one-pound notes. "Oh, of course you can let me have them back."

"It's very kind of you," Billie responded, with real gratitude in the glance which she gave to the one whose sympathy had been spontaneous and sincere. "It had placed me rather awkwardly. Of course, Mr. Risdon didn't think."

The Hon. Peter expressed no opinion upon that.

Billie went on: "If you'll let me have your address, I'll send it to you as soon as I get home."

The Hon. Peter said that there would be no need to trouble. "I think I've noticed you're often here. Any time you happen to see me will do."

"Yes, we come here sometimes. But I'm not sure that we shall again." The Hon. Peter did not appear surprised at that. He produced a card. Billie read it as she slipped it into her bag: 17 Rivers Square. Not the address at which he was commonly known. Not that which the telephone book or the directory gave. But it is no crime to have more than one address, or to pass a card so that its face is not visible to a lady seated at your right hand. She said: "My husband shall return it to you himself in the morning. I think he ought to apologize."

She spoke with the mendacity which her new profession must teach her to practise. She supposed she had done with Albert now. She intended to go herself. The Hon. Peter did not look pleased. "It is to you he should apologize, not to me," he said reasonably. "It will be all right if you post it."

The face of the head waiter had become expressionless. He still thought it was a fishy affair. But the bill was being paid. There was no more to be said. The Hon. Peter Boyle was a valued guest, and one who tipped well enough. He retired discreetly.

Billie sat down while her own waiter went for change. He came back to see her gather it from the plate without leaving the florin which he was accustomed to get. He could hardly be surprised at that!

"Madam will take coffee?" he asked with renewed obsequiousness.

"Madam will take nothing more here," she replied sharply, and thought next moment that she was unfair. The incident must have appeared phoney, which was just what, in fact, it had been. She had no right to resent any indignity which she had deliberately brought on herself. She laid a two-shilling piece by her plate as she rose to go.

She thanked the Hon. Peter again with her eyes, and received his friendliest, smoothest smile.

"She looks too good for that bounder," he said, as she passed out of hearing. "It's queer how some women marry the men they do.... I wonder whether I shall see that two quid again."

"I don't think," the woman who was infatuated by him replied, "that some women have much judgement where men are concerned. But I feel sure that she'll pay it back."

"I dare say you're right," he replied carelessly. An idea moved dimly in the back of his mind. "Risdon's the name. I suppose I could find out who they are," he thought. "But it's not likely that it would be worth while. Almost certainly not.... And if she does send it back, she'll probably put her address."

CHAPTER IV.

THE POLITENESS OF PETER BOYLE

"THE Rivers Square flat," Inspector Cauldron said, "is a place he's had since his college days. He uses it, on and off, to entertain the less-reputable of his lady friends. We've no reason to suppose that it's being used for the dope business. Probably not. He had it long before he met Mildew. We've had it watched since we've taken him in hand, and he hasn't been there as much as once a week, and no one except the tradespeople have been calling. Besides that, we've had the telephone tapped, and it hasn't been used except that he's rung up the housekeeper once or twice for quite natural reasons. The trouble is that if you call there you won't be likely to find him in."

"I might telephone to say I'm coming."

"And you think, if the housekeeper told him, he'd arrange to be in? Well, perhaps he might. But it wouldn't do, because the telephone number's not in the directory, and he'd wonder how you'd got hold of it."

"Then you've got to watch when he goes there, and let me know."

"Yes, I suppose we must. And you've got to be ready to go sharp. He's not got the flat in use now, and if he looks in, it will probably be only to pay the housekeeper, and things like that, and he might be gone in an hour."

"Well, I must just hang about ready. It seems it's the only way."

"I don't like it. I wish you could have gone on meeting him at Staccato's."

"Well, I couldn't. Not after Albert's behaviour there. If you'd got me a better husband—"

"You must thank the superintendent for him. But we all think he did splendidly.... All the same, I don't like you going alone to that flat."

21

"I thought married women could go anywhere. And *of course* I must go alone.... I suppose I might take a baby. It's something that a married woman's quite likely to have."

"Don't be absurd. I don't think you see how serious the whole thing is."

"Not after all I've been through before? You must think I'm dense. Of course, we know he's a murderer, and I don't suppose there are many things he wouldn't do. But I'm quite serious when I say that I don't think there's any risk in calling there to pay back the loan. It's not a place he'll want to advertise with any scandal or row, and from what you say nobody who knows me is likely to be going there, and there'll be nothing strange about a lady the housekeeper doesn't know ringing the bell.... The curse is that we don't know how long we shall have to wait before I can go."

This conversation took place at Scotland Yard on the morning after the Hon. Peter had come to Billie's rescue so generously in the presence of the lady he sought to charm, and it turned out that the waiting would not be long. For on the following morning Billie, having finished breakfast an hour before, was idling time in her own rooms, as she had been persuaded reluctantly to do, when the telephone rang, and she heard Inspector Cauldron's voice at the other end of the wire: "Can you be ready to go to Boyle's flat in ten minutes from now?"

"Say three?"

"Ten's better. It will be time enough, and we don't want you to leave the house until there's some protection for you outside."

Billie made no protest at this, though she thought her present danger was not great. It was true that, while the Hon. Peter might not suspect her as Mrs. Risdon, he might still have given orders for the removal of the young woman who had brought his late chief under the notice of the police, and had done so much harm in other directions to the profitable operations of the gang he now ruled. She knew, therefore, that she must walk in a double danger, either that he might identify her in her assumed character, or be arranging for her destruction in her proper person even though he might not suspect the deception which she was practising upon him. But now that Eustace had gone to Paris, where he had the prospect of obtaining an appointment which would remove him to the remote safety of Anatolia, she had gone herself, at Inspector Cauldron's urgent advice, to a little flat in St. John's Wood, the arrangements and transit having been conducted in such a manner that it was certain that she could not have been followed, and probable that she would not be easy to trace.

She had almost given up calling at Scotland Yard, and had promised not to go out without giving sufficient notice on the telephone to the local police station to allow of her being unobtrusively watched.

Now she learned that Boyle had telephoned his house-keeper a few minutes earlier to enquire whether she had had any letters or callers, and on receiving a negative reply had said that he would be coming round in an hour's time.

The enquiry concerning callers was of no certain significance, and the projected visit might have no relation to herself, but there was an opposite probability. Might he not he going to a place which he did not visit frequently for the particular purpose of instructing the woman as to her course of action if a Mrs. Risdon should ring the bell? It was an idea which might have sinister rather than pleasurable implications, but nothing could go beyond an uncertain guess, and her object being to gain the acquaintance and confidence of the Hon. Peter, she must not be less than content that the occasion had come.

In spite of the slight delay caused by a prudent change of taxis in Oxford Street, she was at Boyle's door within half an hour of receiving Inspector Cauldron's message. As she pressed the bell, she was conscious that she felt nothing of the timidity, approaching panic, which had disturbed her as she had been on the threshold of other, perhaps less dangerous, interviews, and which had only left her as the moment of conflict came.

She had the confidence of a legitimate errand, however its occasion had been contrived. She knew that, whatever interest Boyle might take in the question of how she would return his loan, he could have no expectation that she would be coming at that particular time. She saw also that it was extremely unlikely that even those members of the gang from which he kept so scrupulously aloof, but with whom he must have an inevitable minimum of personal contact, would be invited to, or perhaps even know of the existence of, this private flat, which he reserved for assignations of another kind. There might, indeed, be few places in which she could procure a surer momentary safety, even though he should know her for whom she was.

As she indulged herself in this pleasant confidence, the door was opened by an elderly woman of a sour severity of aspect, which did not relax at the sight of her visitor, or in response to the deliberately smiling manner in which Billie asked if she might see Mr. Boyle.

Billie judged that the Hon. Peter's lady visitors must look to him for any cordiality of reception they might hope to find. Not that the woman appeared hostile. She was of a negative coldness. Not sufficiently alive to have any criminal potentialities. Not likely to be called a lady, but one to whom the invidious "ladylike" might be applied.

"You have an appointment?" she asked indifferently.

"Not exactly. My name is Risdon—Mrs. Risdon. Mr. Boyle is expecting me to call—or to hear from me. He'll know what it's about."

"You'd better come in."

She showed no sign of recognizing the name, and Billie, assuming the instructions she had received, had a moment's doubt of whether she had made a correct judgement of the mask-like face; but it might be natural enough. No doubt Boyle knew her well enough to judge how much or how little should be said to secure his ends.

The woman led her along a softly carpeted passage, knocked perfunctorily on a closed door, entered with the words, "A Mrs. Risdon to see you, sir," and withdrew as Boyle rose from a low fireside chair to receive his visitor.

"This," he said, with smiling emphasis, "is an unexpected pleasure."

"I hope you didn't think that I should forget to return the loan."

"I didn't know you would come yourself."

"It seemed the best thing to do.... I'm fortunate to have found you in."

"Yes; you certainly are. It's not often I'm here at this time of day."

"Then I'm all the more fortunate." Billie had drawn two pound-notes from her bag as these exchanges took place, and laid them on the table. Boyle had drawn forward a chair. "Please don't stand," he said.

"I don't think I should stay," she replied, but with hesitation in her voice. It was a hesitation deliberately assumed. She had no intention of making an immediate exit. She had seldom felt more at ease, more completely mistress of a situation and of herself.

He was equally sure that the interview was in his hands, to be controlled as he would. But though equally at ease, he was more puzzled than she. Why, and in what attitude to himself, had this personal visit been made? He had not doubted that her own part in the restaurant scene had been genuine. He had not the faintest suspicion of whom she was. But he was disinclined to believe in the performance which Risdon had put up. Was she unsuitably married to an impecunious bounder? Had she made this needless personal call with some vague hope that a friendship might develop? Was it possible that it would be a relief to her if she could leave with those two notes still in her bag?

He had seduced several women of his own class, which had been an easier matter among those with whom he associated than would have been the case in more self-respecting circles. He had bought those who had money enough of their own, but desired more. He had learned the power of money rather than its limitations.

It was not strange that he should be attracted by one who was attractive both by his own standards and better ones than he was accustomed to use. And there was the confusingly alluring fact that she was not acting exactly as one of her nature, whether married or single, would be likely to do.

He said: "But you sent your taxi away.... If you will wait a few minutes I shall be able to drive you home."

"I'm afraid I can't let you do that.... Mr. Risdon doesn't know I have come.... In fact, he doesn't know that I had to borrow the money."

"But he must have wanted to know—"

"No. I might have had enough with me. I don't think he thought about it at all."

Billie had taken this line of explanation under the necessity of instantly finding some plausible excuse for declining the offered lift. Actually, she did not know with exactness where Risdon lived. She went on quickly, in determination to turn the conversation her own way rather than follow his: "I wonder how you knew that I'd sent the taxi away?"

"I happened to be looking down into the street at the time."

"I see."

In an absent-minded manner, as they talked, she had taken the proffered chair, and he had resumed his. He leant forward, offering his cigarette-case, which she declined. "I'm afraid I don't smoke," she said, with a smile.

"No. I should have remembered noticing that," he replied, surprising her for the first time, for she had not supposed that she had been observed with such particularity from the adjoining table. He added: "Pity. You don't know what you miss."

"No. How could I?"

"Then why not try...? You'll take a drink, anyway?"

"Thank you, but it's a bit early for that, isn't it...? I really ought not to stay." She had pulled off a glove in an idle gesture as she sat, and she now began to draw it on, as though preparing to go. He said abruptly:

"What does your husband do? I mean, what occupation is he?"

"Oh, he's something in the City."

"Most men are."

"I don't know more exactly than that."

"You needn't tell me, if you don't want to. I only thought I might have been able to put something in his way. I know a good many—"

"I don't see why you should think of that."

"I'm not sure that I do myself." He smiled at her as he said this, as one amused if not puzzled by his own mood. There was genuine admiration—friendly, or something more—in the eyes that were fixed upon her. But she thought that the glance was hard and calculating under its geniality. Was she prejudiced, she wondered, by what she knew, or did it enable her to see truly where she might otherwise have been duped? But anyway, he could be nothing to her. Nothing, at least, but what she meant him to be.

She rose, feeling that she must not be too obviously responsive to that which his words and manner implied. She saw clearly that to draw back was to draw him on, and on to ground which would be safer for her.

Like the drawn glove, her motion stirred him to a new verbal advance.

"I shan't see you at Staccato's? You said you might not go there again?"

"Well," she replied doubtfully, "after the beastly way they behaved, it's not likely we shall—not unless Albert makes a fuss. Of course, he doesn't know what happened after he left."

It was not quite, she felt, what her reply should have been. But she was confused between obtruding facts and the fictions she sought to build. She was finding the difference between outlining a lie and elaborating it in convincing detail. But her excuse for not being driven home, and her evasion of her husband's occupation, had roused no doubt in his mind. No man is so easily deceived as one whose own aim is to deceive, or to overreach. Now he held to the suggestion he had purposed to make, without regard to the fact that she had not said with any certainty that she would not go to Staccato's again.

"Carter's," he said, "Carter's, in Piccadilly, isn't a bad place. I go there sometimes myself. Wednesday nights more often than not."

"I don't know Carter's," she said, with the satisfaction of uttering a truthful word. "But I've no doubt, if you say so, there's a good meal to be got there.... But I *must* go now."

He looked hesitantly at the money on the table, and decided that it might be a mistake to make a difficulty of its acceptance.

He played a more cautious card. "I hope you didn't have to come far to bring that money.... You see, I've no idea where you live."

"Perhaps," she said enigmatically, "it's just as well that you don't." He could make what he would of that! "But if I should happen to try Carter's, you say Wednesday's a good night to choose?"

"Yes. I don't think you could do better than that. Shall we make it a promise for Wednesday next?"

"No. I couldn't promise. But I don't say that I shan't be there."

She left with a feeling that she had done well enough, though she had become more conscious of the difficulty, and of some distasteful features, of the part she had elected to play.

CHAPTER V.

A SECOND RESTAURANT SCENE

THERE could be few things surer than that Billie would be at Carter's Restaurant on the next Wednesday evening, though neither she nor those to whom she made her report were blind to the danger of what she did.

"You've got to work fast now," Superintendent Backwash said, with the slow deliberation which so delusively concealed the agility both of body and mind of which he would be capable when a moment for action came. "You can't say that Carter's is a place of bad reputation. A lot of the best people go there, and its management wouldn't allow any loose conduct. Their licence is worth too much to them for that. But a lot of others go there, whom they couldn't keep out if they would. Mayfair playboys, and—well, a lot of those we haven't handled till now, but may be inviting to give us a call here tomorrow if not today.

"It's just the place he might choose for a cloakroom word, or a slipped note to a man he didn't meet anywhere else, and the fact that he's most often to be found there on a particular day—if that's true—makes it more likely still.

"You can't work too fast now, if you mean to get us the goods, or come through with a whole skin.... We don't want you to take any more risks than you can help, or go on a minute more than you must. But if you can gain his confidence enough to get us a single link—a name or the method by which he keeps in touch with his brother thugs—we'll call you off and work on it our own way."

"I don't mind doing anything really necessary. It sounds silly to talk about dropping it just when I should have—"

"I don't care how silly it sounds. I wasn't only thinking of you. Don't you see that if he tumbles to who you are it tells him we're on his track, and the job's going to be twice as hard as it is now? That's why Tolbooth told us we might be mugs to put you on it at all.... But

I don't say even he really thinks that. You've done well so far—done well every time, and it's more likely than not that you will now."

Billie, hearing this, wished she were equally sanguine, but though she was normally of a buoyant mind, she did not like the way in which she had been praised. It was good in itself, and yet had an ominous sound. No one *always* succeeds. She must hope that the law of averages would not intrude....

She entered Carter's with eyes that were as alert for the presence of others as for the man whom she went to meet, though there was little protection in that, for she was too likely to be known by those whom she did not know. But all the faces were strange to her, until she saw Boyle seated at a table for two in a far corner of the room. The vacant chair was tilted forward, as for an expected guest, which was a dubious invitation to her; but they recognized each other at the same instant, and he rose to adjust the chair to a more hospitable angle. There being unmistakable meaning in that, she went forward confidently.

"You made sure I should come?" she said lightly, as she took the seat, with no more formal greeting.

"I thought you would be glad of a change."

She admired the neatness of the reply, with its suggestion that her husband was one of whom it must be easy to tire; and other implications, of which she could make more if she would. She was most alert at this moment to judge whether he had any suspicion of her, but she was foiled by one who was practised to control expression. Her thought was: "I can tell what he wants me to think; but I don't know what he's thinking. I never should." Perhaps it would be better, even if more dangerous, so. It would be beastly to establish any real intimacy with a man, and then betray him to the law, though he were the worst criminal walking loose in the London streets. As it was, the question could not arise. They both played for their own hands. However near they might draw, there would still be a space that they could not bridge. She said: "Oh, I suppose we all get bored at times, more or less," and became absorbed in the menu card which the waiter offered.

She might have been somewhat less fearful of Boyle, if not of the suspicions of other eyes, had she known how little his thoughts during recent days had been directed to the evil gang which Mildew's end had left in his control.

For the time, a prudent policy had reduced its activities, even to a point at which its income languished and many of its customers suffered the pangs of deprivation from their accustomed drugs. It was a position which had allowed him more leisure to think of her.

He had a fixed and well-pondered purpose, if she should come, as he thought she would, of questioning her concerning the conditions of her present life sufficiently to judge whether he would find it easy to persuade her to leave an unsatisfactory husband—or, at least, to be unfaithful to him—on any terms he would think it worth while to make. He did not suppose that their encounter, which had the aspect of utter chance, was likely to have roused any passion for himself, though he did not underrate his own attractions; but there was the fact that she had come herself to return the loan, for which the post would have been a sufficient medium. If she should come to Carter's also, he might reasonably conclude that parley, if not surrender, was in her mind.

And seeing her sitting opposite to him now, with smiling lips, and a hint of controlled excitement in her eyes, of the true cause of which he had no suspicion at all, he might still feel that she was enigmatic, but could not doubt that he was less than disagreeable to her.

On her side she was better prepared than had been the case at their last meeting for the attack that she had had to meet. She had constructed a detailed picture of life with Albert, sordid and dreary, which, had that gentleman been of a more alluring type, it might have been less easy to do.

The Hon. Peter skirmished lightly for a while as the meal proceeded. He learned that she disliked *Widowers' Houses*. They exchanged opinions upon the dancing of Fred Astaire. She found that he had no knowledge of classical music. Then she faced a sudden frontal assault: "I hope that Mr. Risdon won't be missing you tonight? It was very good of him to let you come."

"Albert," she answered deliberately, "doesn't know anything about it. I told him I shouldn't meet him tonight."

"You usually dine out?"

"Albert has never dined at home since we lost the cook."

"An irreplaceable loss?"

"Yes. So far. Albert isn't very easy to please."

"Well, it has been good fortune for me."

She roused herself to the game that she had to play. Her eyes lied their best as she answered: "It's nice of you to say that."

"I always say what I think."

"That,' she thought, "is about the biggest lie that you ever told." But who was she to condemn mendacity while she studied hard in the same school? She answered lightly: "That's a bit more than I'd like to say. I reckon few women would."

"You mean that we should be too much praised for our own good?"

"Oh, it might be the other way! But—"

Her voice broke off abruptly, as her eyes met those of a lady who had just seated herself at the next table. She controlled herself to make no response to the friendly smile she received. Her first impulse, instinctive rather than reasoned, was to deny an inopportune acquaintance. But was it no more than that? It was hard to hope.

"Something gone wrong?" he asked. The tone was of the casual interest that the moment's confusion required, but she felt that his curiosity had been aroused.

"No. It wasn't anything really. I thought for a moment that a crumb had gone the wrong way."

He did not believe her. He made the correct guess that she had seen someone there whom it was annoying to meet. But that was natural enough. Anyone known to her husband might make trouble by repeating that he had seen her there. Seeking to draw her confidence, he said: "It's a small world."

"Yes. I suppose it is. I learnt its size once. And its weight. But I'm afraid I've forgotten both. What made you say that?"

"I thought perhaps there was someone here you weren't anxious to meet."

"Oh, because of Albert? No, I shouldn't care if he knew. Not enough to lose any sleep. But there's no one here that I know. It isn't a place where I ever come. They're all strangers to me."

He still did not believe, but he saw that she had no intention of treating him with a greater confidence. He led the conversation back to the light verbal fencing which had been its tenor before, and she must sustain her part as she best could while considering the implications of the fact that a woman whom she had met in association with a particularly loathsome member of the Mildew Gang was now seated at a table less than three yards away.

It might—it seemed a poor possibility—but it just *might* mean nothing at all. It was true that Mrs. Ashbarton's hotel was not three hundred yards away. Many American visitors to London prefer to dine elsewhere than in the monotony of their own hotels. But she had denied an acquaintance which at any moment might be awkwardly claimed—with a use of her own name which, whether she should deny it or not, must have a deadly suggestiveness to her companion's ears.

It was, indeed, almost certain that Mrs. Ashbarton would try to speak to her—perhaps all the more probable for the blank gaze that she had received. For there was a business bargain outstanding between them. Professor Ashbarton's posthumous manuscripts should have arrived by now from the Princeton University, and she had agreed to edit them for the press. She realized that the lady, though she might be no more than an ignorant and comparatively innocent purchaser of the illicit goods in which Mildew's myrmidons dealt, might still wish to use this opportunity of meeting one with whom she had a business arrangement, and whose disappearance, on that supposition, might be inexplicable to her.

If it were no more than a chance encounter, such an enquiry might be made, even in the hearing of her host, without any fatal revelation resulting, providing that she could be so quick to disclose her marriage—her change of name—that her own would not be mentioned. But that might not be easy to do! It would have been better to say that she had recognized an acquaintance, and then gone over to her table to speak to her. But she had made that impossible by her ill-judged denial that she knew anyone there. Now it seemed that there was no better course than to finish the meal quickly and withdraw, if possible, before the lady should make any further advance.

With a stubborn effort of will, she concentrated her attention upon a host who was now looking at her with speculative eyes. The game might be lost or not, but it was her business to make sure that it should not be so by her further fault.

"You will take coffee?" he was saying. She knew that he had asked he that once already, and made haste to answer with deliberately laughing eyes. "Yes, thank you. The fact is I ought to be getting back, and it's something I should be quite glad to forget. Have you noticed that the less you want time to pass, the faster it seems to go?"

The Hon. Peter avoided a problem in relativity which even Einstein has left unsolved. "I hoped," he said, "that we could have had an evening together. It's not too late for a show."

"Oh, I wish I could! But it's impossible for tonight. I'm simply *bound* to get back. Perhaps some other time—"

"Perhaps you could find your way to see me again some afternoon? I've got some old things that I should like to show you. There's a necklace that's just your style. A bit old-fashioned, but perhaps of no less value—and certainly of no less beauty—for that."

It was a confident approach, almost insolent in the crudity of the reason it gave, and the hinted bribe, and it confused its hearer's mind with a doubt of how it would be most natural for her to react if she were of the disposition that her conduct must seem to show, further complicated by the doubt of whether Boyle's suspicions had been aroused, and whether she were being invited to anything less than a deadly trap. Even if he had not understood the cause of her confusion—even if Mrs Ashbarton were, a stranger to him—how, she asked her self, could she be sure that she would not be denounced in the next hour But against that risk she recalled Inspector Cauldron's opinion that Boyle's private flat would be about the last place which he would be likely to use for, any act of criminal violence—that it was against his practice to be physically concerned in such episodes, so that, if he should know her for whom she was, it might be one of the few places when at least a momentary safety might be secured—and, finally, that the acceptance, of the invitation would not compel her to go! Showing no sign of these crowding thoughts, and with no longer pause than such, an invitation would be likely to meet, she answered: "Oh, I don't know that I could! But the afternoon—if it weren't long. Yes, perhaps I might manage that.... I'm always interested in old-fashioned things.

"Shall we say tomorrow...? As soon after lunch as you care to come?" He smiled, with an appearance of genuine pleasure, and genuine of its kind it might probably be. She noticed, as she had done before, the hardness of the mouth, that no smile could change, but that might have no sinister meaning for her. And her prompt acceptance appeared to have gained her immediate purpose. The Hon. Peter had already called for the bill, scrutinized it with a quick, competent glance, and was settling it with a sufficient though not generous tip, while she was about to rise, when she knew that her effort to retire unchallenged had become vain, if no more than that, for Mrs. Ashbarton stood beside her chair, and said cordially: "I hope you'll forgive me bothering you, but I've been trying to get in touch with you for several days, and I don't want to miss the chance now. I've just got the manuscripts from Princeton, and if you could spare a few hours tomorrow, Miss—"

She paused over the name—had she actually forgotten?—it was a mere second, but it was a chance that Billie did not miss. "Mrs. Risdon," she said lightly, glancing down at a ringed hand. "I should have let you know before now."

"Then you must allow me to congratulate you both."

It might be no more than a natural error. Billie thought it best to ignore it. She said hurriedly: "I'm sorry I can't manage tomorrow. But I'll ring you up, and let you know what I can do."

She moved away as she spoke, leaving Mrs. Ashbarton feeling vaguely puzzled, vaguely rebuffed.

The Hon. Peter, watching keenly a skirmish to which he lacked the clue, concluded that Billie was annoyed at an inopportune recognition, but saw no cause for any dissatisfaction thereat. If she were annoyed, it must, he thought, be because she considered that there was impropriety in her being there, or serious reason that it should not come to her husband's ears. The more she was conscious of that the more significant her presence became, and doubly so her acceptance of the invitation to visit him again at his own rooms.

When he put her into a taxi at her request, and, in response to the question of what address he should give the driver, received a hesitant, "Oh, Paddington Station," he concluded that she was elaborating caution. He thought that he was embarked on a particularly interesting intrigue, which was likely to be of no great expense, and practically no trouble at all.

But Billie was left with more doubts than it was pleasant to have.

CHAPTER VI.

BILLIE DECLINES ARMS

"WE don't think," Superintendent Backwash said, with the note of official finality in his voice which suggested that if "we" didn't think anything it would be waste of time, if no worse than that, for anyone else to do so. "We don't think it's at all likely that Boyle would know Mrs. Ashbarton, or she him; and the fact that she seems to have assumed that he was your husband after you'd called yourself Mrs. Risdon supports that view.

"Mrs. Ashbarton' has' been buying drugs for the last two years, not for herself, we believe, but for an invalid brother who's desperate to get them, as these addicts become. She paid a high price, so that it was worth Wellard's while to supply her himself, which he could do without risk or trouble, as they frequented the same hotels. We think you've done very well, and you can just put the woman out of your mind.

Billie received this information with no evidence of gratitude or relief. "I wish," she said, "I didn't know differently."

"What do you think you know?"

"Oh, not that! I expect you're right about Mrs. Ashbarton. I meant about having done well. What you say only makes me feel sillier than I did before."

"I don't see way it should."

"I wish I didn't. Don't you see that I ought to have gone to a show with him, as he proposed? And ought *not* to have let myself be rushed into saying I'd go to his flat today? I ought to have got friendly *slowly*, and made him run after me. I just lost my head or my nerve—unless you can't lose something you haven't got."

Superintendent Backwash was surprised by the bitterness in her voice. He saw that she was seriously disturbed by the direction in which the event was developing, and he could not deny that there was reason in what she said. He had a passing thought that it was well that Inspector Tolbooth was not there. His manner changed as he said: "You've got plenty of both. You were confronted by a very difficult and unexpected position. I still say you did very well. But if you feel it's too risky to go to his flat today, you've no need to. It might do him good to wait and find you didn't turn up."

"Oh, I shall go now! I won't shirk facing the mess I've made. I might lose my nerve worse than; I have if I should do that. I've got to find a way through."

Superintendent Backwash made no further protest. He opened a drawer in his desk, and drew out a small silver-mounted revolver.

"It looks a toy," he said, handing it across the desk, "but you're bound to have something you can put into your bag without making it bulge. I can't offer you the weapon we serve out to the flying squads. And it isn't quite what it looks. If you're having trouble you'll find it will change the subject quickly enough. I ought to tell you it's loaded now."

"It's awfully good of you," Billie answered, with a suitably grateful smile, but holding out no receptive hand, "but I don't think I will. I never handled such a thing in my life, and it would go off at the wrong time, more likely than not. Besides, look how it would give me away if it should fall out of the bag!"

The superintendent put it back into the drawer without argument. "I've always said," he remarked, "that you're a sensible girl."

Feeling less assurance on that point than she would have been glad to have, Billie got up to go. "I'll phone you first thing in the morning," she said, "how I got on. Unless you want me to, I shan't come here again till I've got something worth while to tell you, or thrown it up."

Superintendent Backwash observed in his own mind that there was a third possibility, but it was not a thing to be spoken. He said: "The telephone's the best way. And you can rely on us not to be far off, even though we mayn't be easy to see.... Good-bye and good luck."

"Thanks. I expect I shall wriggle through. It's getting something worth having that's going to be the tough job," Billie answered lightly, as she went out. She left a very experienced officer feeling more confidence in her prospects of success than she would have been able to share.

"It's nice of him to wish me luck," she thought, "for there can't be many young women in London this morning who need it more."

CHAPTER VII.

An Unfinished Sentence

FEW things happen in accordance with anticipations. It is improbable that anyone will observe the course of their own lives, or surrounding circumstance, without endorsing this conclusion. But Billie, even had she accepted the abstract truth, would for some time have regarded it as inapplicable to her present experience.

When she rang the bell at the flat, the door was opened by the housekeeper as before, but this time there was no hesitation in her reception. Scarcely looking at her, the woman held the door wide for her to enter, closed it, and with no more words than "This way, please," and still without a direct glance, led her to the room where she had met Boyle before. Subtly, her attitude seemed to say: "I have no part in these matters. I am deaf and blind. I merely open and shut the door."

Billie saw that such an attitude might be consistent either with loyalty to her employer which rendered her indifferent to the interests of those whom he might ensnare, or acute disapproval of what he did. Or mere stupidity might be an equally probable explanation. But there was nothing to suggest alliance or sympathetic support, be her predicament what it might. Practically, she would be alone with Boyle in the flat.

And now the Hon. Peter was holding out his hand with his most ingratiating smile, and his voice was almost gaily triumphant as he exclaimed: "And how good of you to come so early! I was afraid you wouldn't be here for half an hour yet—even if you hadn't forgotten to come at all!"

"I'm afraid I made a rather rash promise. I was bothered lest you might think me rude, going off so quickly after dinner. But if I make one, I like to keep it."

"Well, anyway, you're here now." His tone said more than his words. It was exultant, possessive, giving her presence a significance which she emphatically did not wish it to have. She saw that the interview was likely to be quite as difficult as her fears had forecast.

He went on: "I'm afraid Mrs. Jepson's made the room rather warm. she always is one for a good fire. But you can slip your coat off in the guest-room—it's the second door down the passage on this side. You'll find everything you're likely to want there. And I'll have something to show you when you come back."

"Oh, I don't feel it so hot as all that! I don't think I need take anything off. I shan't be here long enough—"

"You'll stay for a cup of tea, anyway. I told Mrs. Jepson to have it ready for us for four o'clock. I couldn't face her if you went off before."

Billie thought: "What a clumsy liar you are!"—which may have been unfair, for her own conduct was of a misleading kind. But in the next second she recalled the purpose for which she had come. How could she be sure that there was nothing she might discover by a quick search of a guest-room where she could expect at least a few minutes' privacy?—where it was almost certain that she would be able to lock or bolt the door? Not, perhaps, a particularly likely place for the discovering of anything such as it would be useful to her to find—but still, you never know!

"Well," she said hesitantly, "I didn't think of staying that long, but I don't see why I shouldn't. Bert won't be likely to be phoning me before six.... And the room *is* rather hot."

He stepped to the door to open it for her. He thought: "She's a bit awkward. I doubt whether she's ever done anything like this before. And she isn't sure either of herself or me. It's a case of making up her mind for her, and I don't know that I need lose overmuch time about that."

His eyes went to the inexpensive, well-chosen coat which he had proposed that she should discard. He said boldly: "I was always puzzled by the contrast between how you and your husband dress. It's one of the biggest puzzles of life how some girls marry the men they do."

"It cost just three guineas at a small shop in Poland Street—if you know where that is," Billie answered, with a sharp note in her voice, as she passed through the door. She believed, as most women do, and with more reason than most, that she dressed well, but she had contrasted the cost of her own clothes with that of those which Boyle's other feminine dinner-guests had worn, and she asked herself, with as near an approach to envy as it was her nature to feel, why it was always the women with the worst figures who have the most money to spend upon them. She was not even sure of his sincerity. She thought: "He thinks he's just flattering a fool for his own ends." No one likes to be thought a fool, even though their own actions appear to invite the word.... Thank heaven there was a bolt to the door.

The room she entered was a very comfortable bedroom, rather overfurnished, and evidently laid out to meet the needs of feminine guests—particularly such as might have no luggage, and perhaps no purpose of staying when they arrived.

So she saw, as she threw off her coat and hat, and gave a tribute to the mirror, which was little more than a glance, for her mind was on other things, more urgent, if not more important, than that.

For some swiftly moving minutes she searched with the barren result which reason might have warned her to expect. She opened drawers which were filled with underwear of attractive patterns and qualities, and rummaged through them with an abrupt disregard for their welfare such as they would not often receive from feminine hands. But what of Peter Boyle, and particularly of his criminal activities, could she expect to discover here? It was absurd, she told herself, with angry impatience, as the search proceeded. "The fact is," she thought, as her hand went into the empty pockets of half a dozen dressing-gowns, of various sizes and colours, that a wardrobe contained, "I'm trying something that I'm not equal to do. I don't even know what I ought to try at, or how to begin."

She finished at the dressing-table, pulling out drawers which contained toilet-requisites in abundant variety, with an action which had become perfunctory, and eyes that strayed to the glass, when her hand encountered a half sheet of writing paper, folded over and creased, as though it had been hurriedly thrust in, or pushed about among other things.

It was blank on the outside, but she saw some words in a rather large, ill-formed writing: "Don't trust Mr Boyle. He will promise anything and then dr—" So the scrawl ended with an unfinished word, as though the writer had been interrupted and put the paper hastily out of sight. Interrupted, evidently, as she had been writing a warning for anyone who might be in danger of an experience through which she had gone.

But what was the unfinished word? Drench—drain—drivel—dress—no, all absurd. Drink? *Drug?* Yes, that was it. And suddenly there came to Billie an appalling realization, and a sharp fear. Head as Peter Boyle was of a great gang of traffickers in illicit drugs, what opportunities of acquiring these subtle poisons must be his! Not only drugs that produced death or insensibility, but those that would loosen self-control, that would break the power of the will, or from which criminal tendencies, all forms of moral degradation, even insanity, might result. Drugs which could reduce a man or woman to conditions that were literally worse than death. *And he had asked her to stay to tea.*

It was with some difficulty that she controlled an instinct for instant flight, which would have been to fail with ignominy, perhaps with no cause at all. The warning might be no more than the delusion—perhaps the self-persuasion in self-defence—of a hysterical girl. And she was warned now. She would be on the alert, as he would have no cause to suspect.

Besides, why should he try to drug her, if she seemed likely to be complaisant on easier and more satisfactory terms? She must control herself to play this game in the right way. After all, her search had not been fruitless. It had justified her decision to use the room.... She thrust the scrap of paper into her bag, and came back to the mirror. She raised her hands to her hair.

CHAPTER VIII.

ABOUT BEING POISONED AT LUNCH

"I THOUGHT," Boyle said, rising with mechanical courtesy as she returned to the lounge, "that you would never come." His tone implied that the waiting had been hard to endure. She had no reason to doubt that his pleasure in having her there was genuine of its kind. Indeed, unless he knew who she was, what possible motive could he otherwise have? The essential false-hood, with whatever justification, was hers, not his. But she was subtly conscious of a difference in his voice. Of a disquiet, as from a discomfort of body or mind, which was distracting him from full concentration upon the pleasure the moment held. It was as though he might have heard some bad news on the telephone while she had been out of the room. Or was it that he was aware that the moment approached for some act of treachery or violence towards one whom he knew for the fool she was, and that his nerves were not entirely under control? It was a disquieting thought, but it did not greatly disturb her mind. She did not think it was that.

He took no further notice of her for the moment, beyond slightly adjusting a chair for her toward the fire. He sat down on the other side of the hearth. He said abruptly: "I've asked Mrs. Jepson to bring in tea as soon as she can. We'll look at the jewellery after that, if you don't mind. I thought you might prefer it."

"Yes. I shall like it that way."

It was early for tea, but she was not likely to worry about that. If he would continue to sit on the further side of the fire while the minutes passed, she was well content. Perhaps she could lead conversation in ways which would draw him out to talk of his own affairs. It as for that she had come, and so far, toward any real intimacy, she was conscious that she had made no progress at all.

Had it been her mistake that she had not tried to lead the conversation in directions she would like it to take? But it would not be easy to do! She saw clearly that he was one of those who might go far with a woman without exposing his own affairs. His inclination would be to reward her in what he would suppose to be the expected way—not in confidence, but in cash. Was it not equally likely that she would learn more if she should appear incurious of his affairs? To act the ill-mated fluttering fool that he thought her now? Probably it might—if she could play her part in a sufficiently leisurely manner, and were prepared to go much further than she was. But, as the facts were, she saw that she must use opportunities which might not recur.

She had time enough for this doubt while he remained silent for a long minute, gazing into the fire; and she was considering how she could open conversation which might lead him to talk of his own affairs when he asked abruptly: "You don't get on well with Risdon?"

"I haven't found him to be very considerate."

He moved uneasily, as though seeking a more comfortable position in a chair in which comfort should not have been hard to find. And then, after another pause and still without looking toward her, asked, with some abruptness: "Ever thought of making a change?"

This was a different approach from anything Billie had expected to have to meet. But it was not only surprising. It was puzzling in a vaguely disquieting way. It was not natural. Not natural, at least, from the man that she believed Peter Boyle to be. But she answered lightly: "Oh, I don't know! One thinks of all sorts of things."

He turned his eyes on her as she said that, and it seemed to her that they were those of a man who struggled with a great fear. "Yes," he said, "one thinks of all sorts of things."

As he spoke, Mrs. Jepson entered the room. She drew up a small table, and set it out, putting the teapot on Boyle's side, and he turned slowly, and poured out the cups with no more words than: "You take sugar? Yes, I remember that." As he passed her the cup, a telephone rang at the other side of the room.

He rose, as though reluctantly, or still with some rheumatic complaint, and she heard him answer: "Yes.... No, I don't think I can.... Wait a moment. I might hear you better on another line." With a murmured word of apology, he went out.

It was simple to guess that he did not wish her to hear the conversation. But that might easily be, without implying that it was in reference to her. She had a more puzzling problem in his behaviour during the last half-hour. The fear of the warning she had received returned to her mind. Had he been trying awkwardly to pass the time till she should be poisoned or otherwise drugged? No, she told herself, that was no—certainly not the full explanation. There was something going on that she could not grasp. It might have been evident to the omniscience of Superintendent Backwash, but it was not so to her!

Still, there could be no harm in a simple precaution. It was true that both cups had been poured from the same pot. But something might have been inserted in hers too adroitly for her to see. Or there might have been something in the lump of sugar he chose from the bowl. Or suppose he should leave his own untasted while she would drink hers? Anyway, it would be no harm if he hadn't, and if he had it would serve him right! Quietly and quickly she leaned forward and changed the cups.... She had noticed that he took sugar himself. What difference could he detect?

He came back a moment later, looking even less animated than before. He said: "I'm sorry I was called away. You shouldn't have waited." The words came in an impersonal mechanical tone, as though he spoke to the room rather than to her.

He sat down, picked up the substituted cup of tea, and drank greedily. He choked as though it were of some noxious quality. He seemed to find difficulty in swallowing, but persisted in the attempt until he put down the empty cup.

She saw his face turn grey with terror. He was looking straight at her now with the eyes of a hunted beast. Her own may have held an almost equal horror. It was fair, of course; but she hadn't really meant to do that!

He said: "I've been poisoned. I know the signs. There's no hope, unless—" He looked at her in a speculative way, as though he saw her for the first time. She thought that a flicker of doubtful hope came to his eyes. She said foolishly: "You must have had my cup."

He stared at her, as though not comprehending what she could mean. "Your cup?" he echoed. "There's nothing wrong with the tea. But I'm getting unable to swallow. I'm finding it isn't easy to move. I tell you I know the signs. I've been afraid for the last hour. I shan't be able to move soon. I shan't be able to talk. I shall be dead by ten o'clock, unless something's done. And there's only one thing—"

"I'd better get a doctor at once."

"It wouldn't be any use. Shorter's done it, and there's only one man besides him who's got the antidote. In this country, anyway. There's plenty of it in the wilds of Brazil, and Indians who know what it is. But that's no help to me."

"You'd better give me this man's address, and I'll put the police on him at once."

"It wouldn't be any good. And they wouldn't believe. Or if they did, do you suppose he'd admit it to them? We must think of a better way."

"I should say that's the best there is. He wouldn't want to be hanged. When he knows they're on his track, he'll turn up with the antidote quickly enough. I'd better ring them at once."

"Give me a minute first. Let me think. There may be a better way."

He became silent, and she saw that it would be well to give him the time he asked. Certainly there was none to lose if he were to be saved from the fate of which he seemed to have so exact a knowledge, for she had observed that he already spoke, as he had moved, with an unnatural effort, as though a gradual paralysis were already oppressing every bodily function. But certainly also it was well to listen to anything he could still say. To any information he could supply. As much for his own sake (though he might be saved for no better fate) as for the purpose that brought her there.

"Listen," he said. "Do what I ask, and I'll give you any money you want. I'll marry you, if you like, as soon as we can get Risdon out of the way. If you've got the sense and the nerve! But you're the one hope that I have. Jepson wouldn't do it. She'd clear out, if she knew, more likely than not. And there isn't time to— Listen! There's a man who has offices in Bright's Passage—it's off Fenchurch Street on the left. He's an analytical chemist. Webber's his name. But he might be leaving any time now. You'd better phone at once. Royal 4322. Say these words, just as I tell you. Never mind whether they make sense. He'll understand, and wait in: *Mr. Simpson's asked me to say that he'd like the report, if possible, before five o'clock.* Got that? Nothing more. Don't use my name. Only make sure you've got Webber at the other end of the wire."

"Very well. I'll do that."

She crossed the room to the telephone, and got the connection without difficulty. Next moment she heard: "Yes. This is Royal 4322. Yes. Webber speaking." She repeated the words she had been told, and got the reply, after an instant's pause: "Yes. He can have that."

She repeated this as she put back the receiver, and saw, as she went back to the fireside, a faint hope in the eyes of the doomed man. "That means," he said, "that he'll wait to see you. He'll wait till after five, if necessary; but he'll expect you before then."

"He didn't sound at all pleased."

"He wouldn't be. But that doesn't matter. He'll be pleased enough when he sees what you've got to hand over."

With some difficulty, he drew a bunch of keys from his hip-pocket, and passed them to her, selecting one as he did so. "I want you to open that bureau. Luckily there's a cheque-book there. Hurry! There's no time to lose. One of the pigeon-holes on the left-hand side. Yes, that's it."

With the stiffness of movement which was becoming increasingly evident in all he did, he drew out a fountain pen and slowly wrote a cheque. She saw, as he handed it to her, that it was made out to E. Rice Webber, Esq., for £5,000. It was uncrossed.

"You will give him this," he said, "and tell him that I was poisoned by Shorter at lunch today, between one and one-thirty. Tell him the state I'm in, and he'll know the drug that was used. This is his fee, if he saves my life, as I know he can. If he doesn't, it won't be much use to him. I shall make sure that the bank will know before opening time if I'm not alive, and they won't meet the cheque of a dead man. When I've made sure of that, and one or two other things that there's still time to do, I shall get to bed. You'll find me there when you come back, and it rests with you to make sure that I get up."

"I'll be as quick as I can."

"Don't forget to tell him I'll deal with Shorter. He'll have no cause to be frightened of him."

"You think he may be?"

"I know he will. But not as much as he'll be afraid of missing £5,000. It ought to bring him here at a run."

"I'll do all I can."

"Yes. I'm sure you will." He was looking at her with a blending of anxiety, confidence, and appeal, which could not fail to win some pity, even for him. She wondered how he would look if he knew the truth! But she was sincere in her determination to save him, should it lie in her power—and at a risk to herself that he did not know.

As she was passing from the room the telephone rang.

She was at the side of the instrument, and said, "I'll just answer this for you," as she picked it up, taking no notice of his, "It doesn't matter. It'll only be the man who was on before. You'd better leave it to me."

She heard a man's voice: "Mr. Boyle gone yet?"

"No. But he's resting."

The explanation brought a ribald response: "Resting, my eye! Well, tell him we were right about St. John's Wood, and we're dealing with the matter at once."

"Yes."

Conscious of the passing minutes, she hung up hurriedly, repeating the message as she did so.

"Yes," he answered slowly, but with a show of impatient irritation, "they'll know how to deal with her"; and then would have withdrawn or explained his words. But she had already left him for the guest-room, where she caught up her hat and coat, and went out on her errand of mercy.

"So it seems," she thought, as she looked round for a passing taxi, "that they've found out my address, and will know how to deal with me!"

CHAPTER IX.

THE DIFFICULTY OF LEAVING A ROOM

MR. WEBBER'S outer office was vacant. Any staff he may have kept must have left before Billie arrived; but he must have heard her enter, for she had stood for no more than two or three seconds of uncertainty as to how she should announce her presence when the inner door opened, and a man appeared who began to say "Come in," and then pulled himself up, in surprised uncertainty of whom he saw.

"I've come from Mr. Boyle," she said quickly, guessing the cause of his hesitation, that it was someone else he had expected to see. She did not doubt that it was Mr. Webber himself to whom she spoke, though his clothes were shiny with wear, and he was meagre both of form and features. ("Skinny little beast," was her own description of this first impression, when she was able to tell the tale.) Sinister he might be, and physically contemptible in appearance, but he had the air of a man who was on his own ground. Beyond that, she recognized a voice she had heard before.

He looked at her with suspicious eyes. "I don't know you," he said sharply. "I'm not sure that I know anyone of that name. You've brought a message, of course?"

"I spoke to you for him on the telephone less than an hour ago."

"You didn't say so, if you did."

"No. I didn't mention his name. I gave a message that I expect you understood."

"Well, what do you want?"

"Mr. Boyle's been poisoned by Mr. Shorter. He wants your help urgently. He says that you're the only one who can save his life. He's willing to pay a fee of five thousand pounds."

He heard the commencement of the statement with a sharp glance of suspicion, but his manner changed as she mentioned the offered fee.

47

"Mr. Shorter?" he echoed doubtfully. And then, with the hint of a sneer in his voice: "I suppose you've brought the money along?"

She was quick of ear and wit enough to catch the slight stress on the "Mr.," and to reply quickly: "He said Shorter. I don't know any more than that."

"Sir James Shorter is a client of mine. You can't mean him. It's absurd. He wouldn't poison a fly."

"I don't know what he'd do to flies. He's poisoned Mr. Boyle at lunch today between one and half-past, and if you don't help him the police will be told that he got the poison from you. It's between that and getting five thousand pounds."

"If that isn't blackmail," he answered shrewdly, "it's a near thing." But the boldness of her reply may have had effect, for he stepped back and said curtly: "You'd better come in, and tell me all you've been told to say, and how you come to be sent here on such an errand. You look to me as though you're asking for trouble, if ever a woman was.

"I'm not asking for anything more than for you to save a man's life. And I've got the cheque here. Mr. Boyle says the bank will pay it in the morning, if he's alive; but they don't pay cheques for dead men."

"You think it's as simple as that! If I do what you want tonight, what do you suppose I shall be doing tomorrow?"

"I've no idea. But it seems to me it's a good fee. It might be worth while thinking it out while you come along."

"I'd better have a look at the cheque."

She passed it over, and saw avarice shine in his eyes. But it was still evident that he was unwilling to do what she asked, and puzzled and suspicious of her, so that he would say nothing that could not be interpreted innocently.

"Suppose," he said, "what you say is correct, and not just a silly idea that your friend's got because his liver's upset by a big meal. Just suppose it is—and I butt in as you want me to do. What do you suppose Sir James would do to *me* on the next day?"

"I don't think you need worry much about that, even if you know he poisons people more lunches than not. He's going to have his mind full of other things. Mr. Boyle would see to that, even if the police don't have a few words to say. The thing that matters is that we shouldn't lose any time now."

They had been standing as this conversation proceeded, for she had followed him no further than a couple of yards into the inner room, expressing in her attitude the urgency of his coming without delay. But he left her, and crossed over to the further side, where there stood a large safe, the most prominent object in a dingily furnished room, unlocked it, and put the cheque away in a cash drawer. She judged by that, perhaps too readily, that the first round of the game was won.

"We can get a taxi outside," she said urgently. "We can be there in about ten minutes."

He was still standing with his back to her, looking through an array of bottles and sealed packets on the upper shelf of the safe, which it might be expected to hold in view of the occupation which he professed.

"In ten minutes?" he echoed. "We shall be longer than that."

"It's only to Rivers Square."

There was a new suspicion in the sharpness of his reply: "You mean Boyle isn't at home?"

"He's at his own flat. One he uses when he entertains friends."

He had turned round now, and was putting some white packets and other articles into a small suitcase. He looked up with a glance of comprehension which was an insult she could not resent. "Oh yes. I understand now. Where he entertains—friends."

He seemed to be able to place her for the first time, and to have one cause of hesitation removed from his mind. But he went on: "I haven't said that I'm coming yet. I'm just getting ready, in case I decide I will. But you mustn't talk about the police. I must have your word that, even if your friend dies, there'll be no dealings with *them*.... It would do too much harm in my business for me to be mixed up in a scandal of any kind."

The motives that prompted Billie's reply were not clear to herself when she attempted to analyse them afterwards, and to explain them to the friendly but critical consideration of Inspector Cauldron; and where she failed, others are unlikely to be more successful.

It may have been partly that she was reluctant to give a deliberate pledge which she would not keep. It may have been partly that resentment at the imputation conveyed in his previous remark—the slightly derisive stress on the word *friends*—inclined her to present herself in a more accurate character. It may have been partly her perception of the nature of the man, equally cowardly and avaricious, with whom she dealt. Yet, when considered afterwards, none of these reasons had a sound of sufficiency, nor was the course she chose easy to reconcile with the obligations of the oath which she had taken when, at her earnest desire, she had been taken on to the staff of the C.I.D. What she did—seeing clearly, as she did not subsequently deny, all that it must lead to in the next minute—was to answer boldly: "I can't possibly promise that. You may almost say that they're here now.

His startled glance was half-frightened; and wholly venomous, as he replied: "I don't know who you are, or what you're talking about. It all sounds nonsense to me. But you'd better clear out before I call the porter, who might be rough."

"It's no use talking like that," she went on, with no less assurance than before, "unless you want trouble for yourself that you needn't have. You can save Mr. Boyle's life, and get a big reward, or you can stand back, and what happens? Either he gets well without your help or he dies. If he dies the police will have your name as the man from whom the poison was bought. You can guess what that will mean for you, and if he lives—well, you can't be surprised if he gives you a reward of another kind!"

"I won't have anything to do with the matter unless I know what you mean about calling in the police."

"I mean the police are in this already. If they weren't I shouldn't be here. The only question is whether you're to come under their notice as the man who does his best to save Mr. Boyle's life, or the one who sold Shorter the poison.

"I never sold Shorter anything."

"Well, gave it him, if you prefer. But I can't talk here for ever. I only want to know whether you're coming or not. But I think you will. You've got too much sense not to. And, besides, the reward's too big."

"I'm not coming because I believe anyone's been poisoned, or for the money. I'm coming to get at the truth, and see whether you know Boyle at all."

He moved round his desk as he spoke, towards where a coat-hanger stood, with the evident purpose of reaching his hat, and for a moment she thought that her boldness had gained its end. But he glanced down on papers with which the desk was littered, and paused to gather some of them together, and thrust them into a drawer, which he locked.

There was nothing in that to reduce her confidence. Rather, it was a sign that he was preparing to leave. But his action uncovered a newspaper cutting, which she recognized as a photograph of herself which had appeared in a Sunday paper a few weeks before, when her dramatic escape from Maurice Beal's burning menagerie had made it of interest to a million readers.

He glanced at the picture, and then at her. It was plain that the idea of likeness had entered his mind. And the significance of it being on his desk was unpleasant.

50

Yet there was little in that which she did not already know. She had already judged him to have a confidential and criminal part in the operations of the Mildew Gang. She already knew that they were, at that moment, actively seeking her, with probably no less than a deadly purpose. But did he recognize her now? Had he shown that he did, she would have gone further upon the path of candour she had begun to tread, with what result it is hard to guess; but she would always maintain that, had he not uncovered that picture, her bold avowal of police connection would have succeeded. She considered that he weighed cupidity against fear, and she had sought to put some of the fear into cupidity's scale.

But he gave no sign of recognition. He put on his hat, saving, as he did so: "We shall have to go out from this door." His hand motioned toward one at the further side of the room, which opened into the passage. "But I must lock the door of the outer office first from the inside."

He passed through the door which divided the two rooms as he spoke. It sounded natural enough, but the smoothness of his tone gave her a vague disquiet. She would have followed him through the door, but it was closed too quickly against her. She could hear him moving in the outer room, and called: "Mr. Webber, don't be a fool! It's better to help us than not. Let's talk it over. You can't fight the police."

But she got no answer. Evidently he had recognized her, and cupidity had become less than fear.

Well, she wouldn't waste time with him. There was the telephone. She wouldn't be shut up there for many minutes after she had called Scotland Yard! But unfortunately it couldn't be done.

He had thought of that as quickly as she, and had switched the connection outside, so that it stopped at the outer office, where she could hear that he was now using it to more successful purpose.

There was one thing in her favour. He had had the service installed in such a manner that he could overhear conversations carried on in the outer office, and that which he had intended as a check on his staff now operated against himself.

She had not been quick enough to hear the number he called, but she heard the agitated excitement of his voice as he said: "You remember that picture you sent me? Well, I've got the original."

"You've got *what*?" came the answer, in a voice that was harsh and hard. "Where do you mean she—it is?"

"It's locked up in my office. What do you want me to do?"

"There'll be someone coming round soon. Is there a mat outside the door?"

"Yes. Why?"

"Leave the key there, and you needn't stay."

"You're not going to—make a mess in my office?"

There was a second's pause, and then the voice, with a harsher note than before: "I suppose I haven't got to tell you I'm not a fool.... You'd better go. There must be plenty of sociable ways in which you can spend the evening."

"The speaker hung up as he said this, and she heard Webber leave the office, heedless of her appeals for a further argument.

She noticed his steps halt as he stopped to push the key under the mat.

Her imagination was, lively enough to appreciate the significance of the hint that he should be "sociable" during the evening hours. He was to provide himself with an alibi if there should be murder done in his office before he should return next morning. And those who had such an object in their advice might be already upon their way!

It was an emergency which might put a spur to the dullest wit, and Billie's wits were not dull. She looked round alertly. The telephone had failed her, but other methods of attracting attention must surely remain! To break the glass of a door! But both these doors were of solid wood. The windows? There were two, side by side. Old-fashioned, small-paned windows, dingy with London grime.

She smashed a pane. Fresher air came into the room than it may often have had. Broken glass tinkled faintly in an area far below. Nothing happening in consequence, she lost no time in continuing the operation. The smashing of one might arouse no acute curiosity, but surely, if they should continue to fall—! She went on rapidly until neither window had a whole pane.

As there was still no sign of any resulting excitement, she did what she might more wisely have tried at first. She pushed up one of the windows, and looked out.

Opposite, not more than twelve feet away, was a blank wall. She could see, when she leant out, the projecting sills of windows beneath and above. Below was a narrow stone-paved yard, containing dustbins, and a short ladder—too short to have been of any assistance to her, even had it been erected against the wall.

She did not hear or see any sign of life, and recognized, with a tremor of fear, that the other offices in the building might have been left for the day.

If there were a resident caretaker he would most probably be on the highest or lowest floor, and she was distant from both. And there might be none. The fact that no one had been roused by the falling glass... She withdrew from the window, by which there was clearly no means of escape, and looked round the room again. Surely there must be some means of forcing the door. If there were, it was not easy to find. An electric heater requires no fire irons. A man who works at a desk requires no tools that are formidable in weight or point.

She might start a fire. She had done that once before in an anaconda's cage. It would be poetic justice to use Webber's papers for such a flare. But when you can't tell how long you may be locked in with the fire—! (It showed how sure of her they were, and of themselves, leaving her locked up with all his private papers. It was not a comforting thought.).

There was a clothes cupboard at the side of the room opposite to the door. It had a lock, but the key was in it. Exploration discovered a dusty, probably long discarded, overcoat, and a walking-stick.

She tried the key in the locked door. It was useless, but it fitted sufficiently to remain in it. Left thus, it would be at least a temporary obstacle to an attempt to open it from the outside. And that was the door of which she supposed that Webber had left the key under the mat. As to the one that opened into the outer office, she could do nothing, the key being in the lock on the further side. But they might not be able to get to that.

The stick was not heavy or large. Webber was a small man. But it was better than nothing. Driven hard into the mouth, or used with vigour across the eyes—Billie was in a vicious mood, as most of us may become if we know that our own lives are at stake.

She took down the overcoat. Might it be possible to throw it over the head of anyone coming in, and escape before he could see what she did? He would be more than half-choked by the dust! What a filthy old thing it was! She supposed correctly that Webber had been too great a miser to throw or give it away.

But it did not seem a very satisfactory plan, even if there should be only one man at the door, and it was probable that there would be more.... Next moment it became certain, for she heard the steps of those who talked as they came along the passage.

CHAPTER X.

MISS WINGROVE WAS NOT COMPELLED

INSPECTOR CAULDRON looked worried.

"She was in Boyle's flat," he said, "for about an hour, and then came out alone, and got straight into a taxi that was passing—"

"Which was just about what you might expect, if she kept control of the interview, as I felt sure that she would. But I suppose you think the taxi was planted to pick her up?"

"No. We've seen the man since."

"Then she probably meant to baffle any attempt of Boyle's gang to follow her, and she's baffled you too. I think she's a useful girl."

It was plain that Superintendent Backwash was unimpressed by his subordinate's anxiety. Actually, his thought was that Cauldron was reducing his own efficiency, and even making it of doubtful expediency to allow him to remain in charge of the Mildew case, by this excessive fussing over a young woman who was particularly well able to look after herself. Conscious of this attitude, the inspector went on, with irritation added to the anxiety in his voice:

"She didn't try to give anyone the slip, as far as I know. We shouldn't have minded that. She drove straight to some offices in Bright's Passage, Fenchurch Street. She told the man to go fast, so that we had some difficulty in keeping him in sight. She paid him off, and went in. That was more than two hours ago. There's no way in or out of that building except the street door, and a fire-escape on to the roof, and we should see her if she used that. Up to twenty minutes ago she hadn't come out."

"Then we may assume that she's still there.... Is that all you've learned?"

"We've had a watch kept on who has gone in or out of the building. A man named Webber, who occupies offices there, left soon after Miss Wingrove went in, and two men went in half an hour later."

"Know anything about them?"

"No. But Riddell said that you'd remember Webber."

For the first time, the superintendent looked interested. "Webber?" he repeated. "That must be the chemist who was mixed up in the Campion case. You may have got something here."

"I'm glad you agree at last. I don't know anything about the Campion case. Must have been before my time. But there's something going on in Bright's Passage we ought to have stopped before now."

"Perhaps you're right," the superintendent conceded, "but it's quite as likely she's got the situation in hand, and we shall just spoil it by bursting in. You've got the place watched, of course...? Well, then, we'd better go together, and if nothing's happened by when we get there we'll go through it."

With these words he rose, though with no appearance of haste, and added, as he pulled on his coat: "Oh, the Campion case! You never heard of it before? How soon these things get forgotten. Doctor in Liverpool charged with murder. Abortionist. No doubt of that. But the case was unusual. No operation. Said to have used a new drug. Woman took it, and died. May have taken too much. No doubt he'd given it to others. Question was what it was, and what it was supposed to be for. Prosecution said there was no doubt about that either. Strange drug used by Brazilian Indians to procure abortion, and obtained from Webber. Webber said he'd only supplied quinine."

"And I suppose it couldn't be proved?"

"I wouldn't go that far. There was no conviction. Tried by Clements, and he gave a very clever benefit-of-the-doubt summing-up, and the jury followed his lead."

"Clements was the judge who went mad and shot himself, wasn't he?"

"Yes. It was about that time that he told a woman at Leeds, when he was giving her the lightest sentence he could, that he didn't think abortion was a matter about which there was any need to make overmuch fuss. But he wasn't certified then. We don't often get a man on the High Court bench like him."

Inspector Cauldron judged that the superintendent was still bitter over the failure of the Campion prosecution, but he was not interested in that. He asked what sort of a man Webber was.

"Webber? Oh, you needn't be getting hot about him. He's the mean, miserly type. Owns about forty houses in Woking, and gave evidence in a coat he might have worn for ten years. He'd steal a crust from a starving child, if he felt safe. But not violence. He's not the sort to knock Miss Wingrove over the head, if that's the worry."

"What about drugs?"

"Oh, I'll give you that! We're after a drug-trafficking gang. But you mustn't overlook that she seems to have gone to him—if she really did go to his office—quite on her own, and he wouldn't be prepared to see her, more likely than not."

They were in a police car by this time, travelling rapidly city-wards, and it was only a few minutes later that they drew up at the western side of Fenchurch Street, where a man who had the aspect of a typical stockbroker's clerk got in beside them.

"Anything happened?" Inspector Cauldron asked, as they began to move, more slowly than before, towards the further end of the street, where Bright's Passage is situated.

"Yes, sir. A few minutes after you left the two men came out again, and Miss Wingrove was with them. They called a taxi, and got in together. Sergeant Riddell followed them. He told me to let you know. I phoned, and was told you were on the way here."

"Did Miss Wingrove seem to be going at her own...?"

"Yes, sir. If she'd wanted to, she could have left them quite easily."

"Sure there wasn't a gun poked into her back?"

"There was no doubt about that. She wasn't under any restraint at all."

"Anyone with Riddell?"

"Yes. He took Doyle and Rogers. He's gone in the private car."

"And we," the superintendent added, speaking for the first time, "can't do better than go back by the way we came."

CHAPTER XI.

"GO WITH HIM, TWAIN"

BILLIE heard the two men stop outside the door. It was too thick and well set for the hearing of lighter sounds, but in a few moments she was aware that a key was being inserted, and that it had met the obstacle of the one that was already there.

She stood close to the door, wishing to hear all she could, keeping very still lest they should become aware of her presence. "If they did," she thought, "they might try shooting me through it. It would be hard to identify anyone who did that...! But the snag would be that they couldn't be sure that they'd done the job properly. Not unless they could have a look afterwards.... No, they'll try something surer than that. I shall be silly if I don't hear all I can." So she recruited courage, but it was not a pleasant idea for a girl to have. She did not move away from the door, but she kept very still.

The men were talking now. It sounded like a dispute though the voices were very low. She could hear nothing of what the one said, but the other was clearer. With her ear pressed to the door she heard: "He wouldn't be such a damned swine." And then: "I tell you, he wouldn't dare. He hasn't got the pluck of a louse." She may have made a good guess that they were discussing whether Webber had fooled them about the key, and that the more audible of her unwelcome visitors was arguing that he would not have dared, in a phrase he was using now, "to make monkeys of us." But to a further remark from his companion, which was as inaudible as before, he answered: "Yes, we can try that first, but you'll find mine's the best way."

She heard their steps recede along the passage, and thought for a moment that they were withdrawing, leaving her in the doubtful security of a room that she could not leave. But they did not go.

She heard them next at the door of the outer office, to which she supposed that they had no key. But she was wrong on that point, for what Webber had put under the mat had been a ring on which both keys had been hung. Their delay in trying it may have arisen from the fact that they had no key to the inner door, which they would know must be locked, without being aware that the key was in it. But now she heard the key turn, and knew that the next five seconds must decide the attitude in which she would meet them.

She made no conscious decision, though her eyes rested for a moment upon a heavy chair, the back of which, tilted under the door-knob, would at least have delayed their entrance, but she showed more wit when she sat down upon it, putting the stick, as she did so, into an umbrella stand, where it would be natural for it to be.

She looked up with a smile as the two men entered the room. "I'm glad you've come," she said gratefully. "But I thought you wouldn't be long. Of course, I heard all that Mr. Webber said on the phone. I think he's just a bit on the silly side. I should have been glad to wait to see you without being locked in.... And he didn't tell you the one thing that matters. I hope he hasn't gone where you can't find him now."

The men she addressed in this easy manner may have been equally surprised, but they reacted differently. The one who had come in first was a plain brute, an outsize in bullies, with cunning eyes grotesquely small in a broad, fleshy face. His nose was a thick beak over heavy lips and large, prominent teeth. As she met a malignant gaze, she realized how foolish it would have been to have relied upon physical self-defence against such an antagonist. She saw also that the attitude she had chosen might have been equally futile had he been the only one with whom she must deal, for his eyes did not change their hostility as she spoke, while his upper lip rose in an ugly sneer.

But the man behind him, of little more than half his size, was of a different kind. Whatever he had expected to meet, and however willing he may have been for his heftier companion to be the first to enter the room, he took charge of the proceedings now, with a ready adaptation to her own tone, though his suavity may have had no more sincerity than hers, or perhaps less.

"We were afraid you'd feel rather sore, being locked in the way you were, but I'm glad you take it the way you do. We got here as quick as we could, and of course you're free to go now any time you like. But what is it we ought to know?"

He pulled forward a chair and sat down opposite to her as he asked this question, and, as she looked at him, she both hated and feared him more than the bully who still stood menacingly between her and the door. He was regarding her with coldly probing eyes in a white, pock-marked face. They were dull eyes of a neutral colour, neither green nor brown, but she did not think him to be dull. She thought that his wits were alertly awake, cruel and cold.

She did not believe that he would let her go, as he said, nor foolish enough to put it to a test which might have brought immediate crisis upon her. But she judged that he was quite willing to hear her talk before they should disclose their own purpose, and it must be her business to say that which would make that purpose more comfortable for herself than it was likely to have been when they entered the room.

"He didn't tell you why I came here. Mr. Boyle's dying, and he's the only man who can save him. If you can't get hold of him, and make him do what's necessary, Mr. Boyle will be dead in about four hours from now."

It was a random shot, which would miss any useful mark, more likely than not. They might know already. They might be indifferent. Or it might even be welcome news. Yet it was her one chance to divert their minds from plans which she felt with a sound instinct were now as bad for her as it was possible for them to be. But she saw now that it was something they had not known, and different from anything they had expected to hear.

The big man spoke at once, while his companion regarded her for a moment in critical silence, as though weighing the probable truth and the implications of what she said. She heard: "Who's Boyle? And what the devil is that to us?" But she kept her eyes on the one on whom her fate, as she felt sure, primarily depended. She remembered the secrecy which Mildew had maintained as to his own identity. Was it possible that these men did not know Boyle? But she remembered that Webber had not been ignorant, and they seemed to be over him. Or at least the one did who was seated opposite to her. He said: "Never mind that now, Humphries. Miss Wingrove has got more to tell us.... What's this about Mr. Boyle? He was all right this morning. And may I ask, Miss Wingrove, what Mr. Boyle is to do with you?"

"Mr. Boyle was taken ill after lunch. He says Sir James Shorter poisoned him. Anyway, he's very ill now. He won't live many hours unless Mr. Webber goes to him at once with an antidote which he's got in his bag."

"I'm not saying I believe you or not. What I'm asking is how you come to know this, and what it's to do with you?"

"I was with Mr. Boyle at his flat when he was taken ill, and I'm doing my best to help him. If you'd only do something, and not waste time!"

She saw as she spoke how confusing it must be to them. They had instructions, probably from Boyle himself, to hunt her down and destroy her, as one who was bringing trouble upon the gang. They could not know that she had introduced herself to Boyle in another name. Could it sound probable that he would be relying upon her in such an emergency? Yet the very fact of such confusion might incline them to delay action against herself until some explanation should be obtained.

"What do you want us to do?"

"I want you to find Mr. Webber, and make him go to Mr. Boyle before it's too late."

"You're very anxious to save Mr. Boyle's life?"

"Anyone would be. When you see a man being poisoned—"

"What makes you think he was? You know it's a very serious charge to make."

"I haven't made it. I've only told you what Mr. Boyle says."

"And Mr. Boyle is your friend?"

"You might say more than that. He was asking me to marry him when he fell ill."

Up to this point she had watched the faces of the two men, and knew that the one who stood silently over her was suspicious and unconvinced. But she had been able to make no guess at whether she were believed by the one who sat opposite, questioning her with such quiet rapidity, or what effect her answers were having upon him. Only now, as she ventured this bold assertion incredulity came into his eyes.

"I don't think I can believe that. I happen to know he had other plans. Suppose I ring him up, and ask him to confirm all you're telling us?"

She saw the danger instantly. What she had said was true, and to appeal to him for confirmation should have been her strongest support. But by what name? As Billie Wingrove he had not met her at all. She might say that he knew her by another name, but how soon would it lead to disclosure that the two were one, with consequences to herself which were easy but unpleasant to guess?

But it would have been fatal to show hesitation. And there was the probability that he would e too ill to answer. There was another attractive possibility. Suppose that Inspector Cauldron had become alarmed for her safety, and had raided the flat? He might be there now!

With no perceptible pause of hesitation, she answered: "Of course I don't mind. I should say it's the best thing you could do. But you mustn't be surprised if he's too ill to talk to you."

"Where do you say he is?"

"At 17 Rivers Square."

"Never heard that he had an address there. Humphries, you might find the phone directory."

"You won't find it there. The number's Tavistock 6099."

"And how are we to know that?"

"I suppose you'll know Mr. Boyle's voice?"

"Who else is there?"

"There was no one except the housekeeper, Mrs. Jepson, when I came away."

"Well, we won't phone from here. We'll have a taxi. You won't mind coming with us?"

"Not at all. It seems the best way. But you don't believe me, or you wouldn't have refused to phone."

"I haven't refused. I said we wouldn't do it from here."

"It's the same thing. You think there's a catch somewhere. If I could only convince you that I'm trying to save Mr. Boyle's life!" (And perhaps my own, she thought, which I value a lot more.) "I suppose you couldn't break open a safe?"

"No. It's not a line of business I should care to cultivate."

"If you could open that safe on your left hand you'd see Mr. Boyle's cheque to Mr. Webber for £5,000. It's to be his fee if he saves him. I brought it to him, and he locked it up in that safe before he got too frightened to go on with the case."

"Frightened of what?"

"Frightened of Sir James Shorter, as far as I could make out. But he wasn't exactly confidential."

"He said nothing about being frightened of us?"

"No. He was trying to make trouble for me, so that Mr. Boyle would be left to die."

She could not tell how far she were believed, nor whether any credence she might obtain would change their purpose toward her. The one man evidently did not know so much as the name of Boyle. It could be nothing to him. The other had a degree of knowledge she could not gauge, but he might prefer to keep clear of the quarrels of those who controlled the gang, or he might be one to whom the death of Boyle would be a welcome event.

Of one thing only she could be sure. There would be no use in appeal to any decent human instinct, for none was there. Unless she could escape them by her own wits, she could only reach them by the passions that had controlled Webber—different from him in many respects though they might be. She must rouse their cupidity or their fear.

But there was one matter on which it appeared that they all felt alike. They were willing to leave the room. Probably they had never meant to do her any fatal violence there, but rather to lure her away to a lonelier place. If that were so, they must welcome her willingness to come with them. And, even so, it was a chance she must take. And, to assure some measure of temporary freedom, she must make them believe that she was without fear, and even anxious to go. "Go with him twain" came to her mind, and the text had a new meaning, and a new force in the wisdom of its advice.

She rose with the thought, and said: "But we're losing time talking here. I don't care whether you phone, or come at once to see the state Mr. Boyle's in, or find Mr. Webber first—though, of course, that would be the most sensible thing to do—but it's silly to waste any more time talking here."

The smaller man, whose name she had not learnt, rose also, but with no indication that he felt any need for haste. He asked "How do you know Webber isn't there now?"

"I don't. I don't suppose he knew himself when he left here. He looked to me to be the sort of man who changes his mind every ten minutes."

"Not with £5,000 to be picked up."

"But if he thought he mightn't live to draw it out of the bank?"

"Why should think that?"

"Because he isn't a fool, if you ask me. Anyway, that's what he did.... But I don't suppose it's the last penny that Mr. Boyle would pay to anyone who would make sure that he'll be alive this time to-morrow. He might think a lot of it if you took Webber there at a run."

"Well, it's a wild tale, and I don't know how much to believe. But I'm sure we'd better find out what the truth is." He turned to his scowling companion as he said this, so that she could not see the look that accompanied it, though she saw that which it roused in the eyes it met, which she did not like. But she still felt that she could play the game in no better way.

CHAPTER XII.

CONCERNING A PISTOL AWKWARDLY PLACED

THEY followed her to leave the office first, following closely behind her. The door of the lift stood open as they had left it. As they approached it, Humphries gave the other man an enquiring glance, and was answered by a slight shake of the head. To have started the lift, and pushed her in, so that she would have been left jammed, half in, half out, and crushed by its arrested power—it would have had an appearance of accident which it would have been difficult to disprove. It may have been the intention with which they came.

Going first, she could not see this evidence that she had won the first round of the deadly game.

As they emerged to the street, the smaller man, whom she had now heard his companion address as Mr. Guttins, turned to her to ask: "You haven't got a cab waiting?"

"No. I paid it off."

"Though you were in such a hurry to get Webber to go back with you?"

"I didn't expect him to come instantly. I knew there'd be a good deal to explain."

"Well, look out for one, Humphries."

The man he addressed had already raised his hand, and a taxi pulled up to the pavement to take them in.

The question Billie had been asked had disposed her to think that there was a genuine intention to accompany her back to the flat, and it was evident that they did not doubt her disposition to do so. This confidence was confirmed when Guttins said: "You'd better give the driver the address, Miss Wingrove"—and the man received her "17 Rivers Square" with a surly but assenting nod.

So she had the moment of potential freedom, and let it pass. There were ten seconds during which she could have turned aside to the crowded street, and it would have been difficult for them to have obstructed her intention without a publicity which would have been fatal to their purpose or to themselves. But Guttins had judged her rightly so far as to conclude that, if she were led to believe that they would go with her to the flat, she would not attempt to leave them. It showed that whatever scepticism he might think it expedient to profess, he had little doubt of the truth of the tale she told.

And so she got quietly into the vehicle, though well aware of the peril of what she did—especially if Boyle should still be sufficiently conscious on their arrival to be informed that Mrs. Risdon and Billie Wingrove were one, and still have authority to enforce his will.

But he might be conscious—or the police might be at the flat, or—there were a hundred possibilities. When the heads of an illegal association begin to poison each other, there must be opportunities for those who would break its power. Billie had work to do which would not be advanced by evading her dangerous companions now. Inspector Cauldron had been quite right when he had said that she had gone with them willingly. Her trouble was that their plans for her were of a different kind. She got in at the back of the vehicle, and Humphries got in beside her, after a word from Guttins she could not hear.

Guttins got in with the driver, to whom he spoke in the same inaudible tone. She would have preferred to hear, but did not conclude that anything he said need be hostile to her. He had a habit of speaking as though the sounds were forbidden to go abroad more than a few inches from the lips they left.

The driver made no answer. He drove westward as rapidly as the traffic allowed.

Humphries took no notice of her. His attention was fixed upon the rear light of the car, through which he looked back continually.

They had turned into Edgware Road, and she was puzzling her mind as to how the driver should consider that the best route for Rivers Square, when Humphries, after a prolonged inspection of the road behind him, said in a voice of anger, and, she thought, something of fear: "We're being followed."

Guttins asked curtly: "C.I.D.?"

"It's a private car."

Guttins rose slightly in his seat to look back. He said something to the driver, who merely nodded in reply.

A moment later the car slackened speed slightly, and then swerved violently. Rotating with two wheels in the air, it joined the traffic on the other side of the roadway, went at high speed for thirty yards and swerved into a side-street on the east side of the road.

For the next three minutes it took no direct course, turning almost every corner to which it came. Then it swung into an open-gateway, in the seclusion of which the driver got out and covered the plates with others of different numbering.

"Guttins turned to Billie while this curious operation proceeded, to say: "I don't know who's following us, but we can do without them; at any rate till we've seen how the land lies."

"Yes," she said "with simpler truth than she had consistently employed, "I can see how you feel."

So she could, and it did not appear to indicate any more immediate menace to her. That they would wish to avoid the police, particularly before they had seen Boyle, and perhaps taken instructions from him, was an easy guess. That they might be in fear of pursuit by hostile members of a gang the principals of which were on no better than poisoning terms was an alternative explanation of almost equal probability. But she had an additional cause for confidence, and reason for keeping still.

The sudden swerve of the car had thrown her violently against its side, with the burly form of Humphries upon her. For a moment he had been a crushing, unpleasant weight. His jacket pocket, pressing against her hand, had bruised it with a hard object the shape of which had been unmistakable, and it had been the work of one quick-witted second, as they had regained equilibrium, to slip her hand in and draw it out. She had been unable to retain it in her hand, but had dropped it backward, so that it was on the seat between them. She could reach it in a moment with her left hand, as he could have done with his right, but she had the important advantage of knowing that it was there.

The car backed out of the opening, and had gone only a short distance further when Guttins looked back to her, and said smoothly: "I think, Miss Wingrove, I can be of more assistance to your friend if I get out here, and get hold of Webber, while you go on to the flat"; and, as he spoke, the car slackened speed at the pavement, and he opened the door and slipped out with an agility which suggested that he had had practice in what he did. The car was moving rapidly again in the next second.

There had been no time for her to protest, or to attempt to alight also, had she wished to do so, and it had been so sudden and unexpected that, for a moment, she was uncertain how to regard it. But as she thought she became afraid.

It was clear that his intention must have been known to his companions; almost certain that he had told them of it in those first whispered words which she did not hear. It was possible that he had gone to seek Webber, who might live in that neighbourhood—but it was unlikely. She began to doubt whether they had any intention of taking her to the flat. She had seen, when the plates were changed, that she was not in a chance-hired taxi, but a car which must have been waiting for them, and driven by one of their own gang. It was with a deliberate effort to sustain her courage that she told herself that two must be less formidable than three, and that she had a weapon they did not guess.

She saw that the decisive question was: "Were they taking her to Rivers Square?" If they were, she could do no better than to sit still. If not, she might find that delay would bring her to a worse position than that in which she now was. She had a vision of the car turning into high gates which closed behind it, so that she would be in a prison which might easily be a tomb. When men of criminal character get control of the huge funds which drug trafficking brings, there can be no narrow limit to what they have power to do. When they are alarmed for their own lives or freedom they will not be scrupulous in the methods by which they think they may save themselves.

She thought: "I've got to find out what they mean to do. If I delay I shall get funkier than I am now." She forced the issue through fear that her courage fail. She said, with a tremor in her voice she could not control, but which must have sounded natural enough to those who heard it: "Are you sure you know how to get to Rivers Square? You don't seem to me to be going the best way.

The driver gave no sign that he heard. Humphries looked at her without replying. His silence, and the fact that the car was now heading north, were sufficient answers. Guttins might be going to Rivers Square, but there was no intention that she should do so. They might have believed her tale, and still seen no reason to alter whatever sinister end had been planned for her; concerned only to obtain any information that she could give, and to use it as a means of getting her to go quietly the way they would. The realization roused her to action, in which, though her heart might be beating faster than she was aware, she was no longer conscious of fear.

She met the threatening, contemptuous gaze beside her with eyes as hard as his own.

"You'd better not do anything without thinking first," she said quietly, "because you might be sorry. I've got something to say to you both, and I'm warning you before I begin. I'm not going anywhere in this car but to Rivers Square. I know, if I tried to cry out, you could throttle me with one hand, and I believe that you're thinking of that now. But a bullet's quicker. I've got a gun in the seat between us. *The least movement, and it goes off.*"

The last words were urgently said, for the man beside her had made a spasmodic movement which he scarcely restrained in time to prevent her hand tightening on the weapon she now held on the seat between them, its muzzle, as he had become aware, pressing against his hip. She held it awkwardly, her arm straight down at her side, and her fingers gripping it round lock and barrel, with no very clear idea of what movement would be required to fire it. But it was not a position in which he would be likely to wish her to experiment on that point, or start a scuffle in which it might instantly discharge a bullet which could not miss.

She went on with more confidence as she saw the effect that her warning gave: "You'd better tell the driver to stop the car, and let you get out. There's no need for you to come with me, and when you're in the street it'll be a lot safer for you. I'm not very used to revolvers like this, and any minute it might go off."

Her words were instant in their effect. Humphries' voice was sullen but hasty as he said: "You'd better pull up, Sinster, unless you want to have a hole in the back of your head"

She was not sure that it was an act of wisdom to let Humphries loose, knowing where she would most probably be going, and able, she did not doubt, to get into speedy communication with his superiors in the gang but she felt unable to endure the prolonged tension of the position in which she sat. The awkward turn of her wrist, which was already aching—the real fear that the gun might go off at any moment, particularly if she should attempt to relieve the position of her twisted hand—the knowledge that an instant's relaxation of watchfulness might mean that the tables would be turned on herself with disastrous consequences—combined in deciding her that it would be better to halve the opposition with which she would have to deal.

"Keep your hand away," she said sharply, in a sudden apprehension that he might make a grab at her wrist, as the big man rose from the seat, revealing how awkwardly her hand, pressed sideways into the cushion between them, had been holding the deadly weapon. But he had no thought but to leave the car with a whole skin. To his mind the danger of the unintentional discharge of a gun which he knew to be responsive to very light pressure was even greater than that of a deliberate action on her part, making him more apprehensive of her than he would have been of Inspector Cauldron in the same position; apart from which she was not requiring him to perform any reluctant action. To leave the car was exactly what he would have chosen to do, now that she had gained a position which rendered impracticable the method of the murder which they had been instructed to commit. "Besides," he thought, "if this Boyle—I wonder who Boyle is?—is one of the heads, and he's been poisoned, there may be different orders by his time tomorrow—or we might find, when we'd done her in, that there'd be no one to pay us off." Very willingly, though with no friendly feeling for her, he got out.

Left alone with her in the car, the driver moved on at a slow pace, and turned his head back to say: "I don't know what all this is about, but I'll drive you anywhere you want to go, if it means there'll be no more trouble for me."

"I'm not going to promise anything, but there'll be a lot more trouble for you if you don't."

"I don't see why I should drive you anywhere while you talk like that."

"I suppose you don't *want* a bullet somewhere about the back of your neck?"

"If you were fool enough to do that, you'd wreck the car, and kill yourself more likely than not.... And you'd be in the dock for murder if you were alive long enough to be hanged."

Billie saw that the position was not without difficulty. She had a well founded idea that she would have no legal justification for shooting him on any pretext of general criminality while he was offering no violence to her, and, however that might be, she knew it to be a thing which she would not do. But she answered boldly: "I could shoot you for resisting arrest; and I'd wreck any car rather than be taken where I don't want to go."

"I'm not doing that. I'll stop and put you down any moment you say the word. All I've said is I won't drive you to Rivers Square unless I know there's going to be no more trouble for me. You can't have me arrested for that."

"What about changing the plate...? And what about where you *were* going to take me before your friend got out of the car?"

"Well, what about it? You hadn't hired me. If you didn't know where you were going, you shouldn't have got into the car."

"I knew where it was supposed to be going, and so did you.... But you can tell all this to Inspector Cauldron. I shouldn't wonder if he'll let you off if you tell him all you know, and it'll help a lot if I say that as soon as that bully got out of the car you drove me to Rivers Square as quickly as you could go."

"Well; I'm doing that now, aren't I? But it's no use asking me to tell things I don't know. I don't know about anything wrong."

"Well, if you can make Inspector Cauldron believe that, it ought to be all the better for you."

The man made no answer, and Billie sat back in a car which was now moving at the highest speed which is allowed in an urban area, and more evidently than before in the direction in which she wanted to go.

Was she doing the right thing? She was less than sure. She might have told the man to drive to New Scotland Yard, and within twenty minutes the control of the event would have been in stronger hands than hers. Or she might have stopped the car at a telephone booth, and given the essential information more quickly still. But that would have been difficult without losing the man she had captured now, which she would have been reluctant to do. And dominant in her mind had been the urgency of getting back to the flat—to the probably dying man—to find out what his condition was. Whether Webber had gone to his assistance. Perhaps, if he had not, to take fresh instructions for bringing him there, even by the coercion of the police.

It was at least, certain that, while she was working to save his life, Boyle would be unlikely to be hostile to her And was it not at least probable that she would reach the flat before Guttins would be there, or perhaps any communication from him, such as would come to the ears of a man in the condition in which she supposed Boyle to be?.

Probably she could phone Inspector Cauldron from a room which would have been left vacant and little time would have been lost. And, at the worst, there was the gun, which she now had in a firmer grip than before. They seemed afraid of that! Perhaps more afraid that she might discharge it through clumsiness than that it would be fired with intent to kill.

Under all was the sense of the urgency of the event. Of the rapidity of the passing minutes. Not that Boyle was one she had cause to love, or whose death would be occasion for grief. But she was not without the instinctive impulse to help anyone who appealed to her in such extremity, even though she knew that he had given ruthless orders for the death of one whom he did not know her to be. And there was the confusing fact that, with whatever legal excuse, she had herself deceived him into the belief that she was his friend.

Such thoughts as these passed swiftly through her mind, which might have been better occupied in planning to meet whatever ordeal the coming minutes might bring upon her. But it is difficult to plan for a position you do not know. A Napoleon of the battlefield might find it hard to forecast his tactics against an enemy of whose numbers or dispositions he was unsure.

Boyle might be conscious or unconscious, living or dead. If alive, he might still regard her as his friend or most dangerous foe. He might be alone and helpless, or in the midst of his murderous gang. Well, at the worst, there was the disconcertingly deadly weapon she held, which they would not find it easy to wrest away. It would certainly go off if they should do that, though the direction of its bullets might not be sure.

And, finally, there was the better chance that the police might be there already. Knowing Inspector Cauldron, she felt this to be a most probable anticipation. And so, feeling rather than thinking these diverse possibilities, she came to 17 Rivers Square, and to the first problem she had to face. What was to be done with the car, and the man now in the seat before her?

CHAPTER XIII.

THE ATTITUDE OF A SICK MAN

SINSTER said, "Here you are," in a sullen voice. He made a motion to rise.

"Sit still," she said sharply.

"I was only going to open the door for you," he replied, more sulkily than before.

"I can do that for myself. You'd better stay where you are."

She had had an idea which might be useless, but was worth trying. Should it fail, she must let the man go. Guttins and Humphries having gone already, there did not seem that there could be much further harm in that. Anyway, she was decided that she would not enter the flat, and face whatever might be before her there, with a dangerous captive already upon her hands. Still, he was her captive, and she was unwilling to let him go. And now she had an idea.

Rivers Square is not a crowded thoroughfare. She looked, for twenty yards, along an empty pavement. Beyond that a rather shabby man in a bowler hat was coming toward them. She considered him as he approached. He took no notice of them. He was not very reputable in appearance. He might possibly be Boyle's watchdog, and an added danger to her. Well, she must risk that! It was not very probable.

She dropped the window as he came up, and called to him: "Would you please come here a moment?"

He responded at once, though with no animation or quickening of pace.

"I've got," she said, "a dangerous criminal here, and I want you to make him drive to Scotland Yard. You can have this." She showed the gun, which she had kept backward at first, not feeling it to be likely to attract a stranger to conversation. "Make him go there, and ask for Superintendent Backwash or Inspector Cauldron.

Ask them to look at the plates on this car, and they'll have something to go on with before they decide what the first charge is going to be. I want you to tell them that Miss Wingrove sent him, and that she's at Rivers Square. They'll know what to do when they hear that."

The man heard this with an expressionless face, but his eyes were alert. She felt she was understood. Without replying, he went round to the back of the car, where his inspection was brief but sufficient.

As he came back he pulled out a card, which he showed her as he opened the front door and got in beside the driver.

"You'd better have this," she said, holding out the weapon which she would not have been entirely unwilling to surrender to masculine hands. But he shook his head. "I shan't need that," he said, speaking for the first time, "but I'll just give him the once-over." He passed rapid accustomed hands over the scowling Sinster while Billie got out of the car; and, being satisfied that he had no lethal weapons upon him, he sat back. "Now, my man," he said briskly, "off we go."

Billie looked after the retreating vehicle with an increased respect for the efficiency of the C.I.D.; and it was in a resultant spirit of confidence, both in herself and the Department she served, that she pressed the bell of the Hon. Peter Boyle's quietly respectable flat. She had shown her efficiency by capturing a member of the gang and sending him to the Yard driving the evidence of his illegal practices. She knew that, within fifteen or twenty minutes, he would be there, and with him the information of where she was, on which she thought that Superintendent Backwash would not be slow to act. She had little fear that anything would happen in the meantime which would be beyond her control.

Her first reception did nothing to reduce confidence. The door was opened by Mrs. Jepson, who looked worried and frightened, but friendlier than before.

"I'm glad you're back, miss," she said at once. "Mr. Boyle looks dreadfully ill to me. It's about all he can do to speak. I'm sure he ought to have someone. But he wouldn't let me phone for a doctor. Not till you got back. He said you'd gone for the only one who could do him good."

"The doctor hasn't been yet?"

"No. I wish he had."

"He ought to have got here before now. You're sure nobody's been?"

"There's a gentleman called a few minutes ago. He said he was a friend, and Mr. Boyle would be glad to see him. I told him how ill he was, and he said he'd try to persuade him to have a doctor sent for at once."

"Was it Mr. Webber?"

"He didn't give any name."

"Is he with him now?"

"I think I heard him go into the lounge just as you rang."

"I expect you did. There's someone telephoning there now."

"I hope he's ringing a doctor up."

"Yes, I hope he is." Billie spoke with sincerity, but her hope was not great. She had a prudent inclination to withdraw, but her mood of confidence won. "I'd better see Mr. Boyle, and tell him what I've been able to do."

Mrs. Jepson led the way to the bedroom. Boyle raised his head as they entered. There was more freedom in his movement and more animation in his expression than Billie had expected to see. Yet it was clear that he was a very sick man, and he spoke with evident difficulty. "I must thank you," he said, "that you got Webber to come."

Evidently that was Webber telephoning in the next room. Almost as surely he had not disclosed who she was. But then he had not expected that she would be here. He thought that he had disposed of her. He might now be leaning what had occurred.

She answered the man who was looking at her with grateful eyes. "I can see he's given you what you needed. You look better already."

"I feel bad enough. But I shall be all right tomorrow if I have the injections regularly till then."

The faint sound of Webber's voice in the next room had ceased. He might be listening, or he might have hung up and be back in the bedroom at any moment Mrs. Jepson had withdrawn. There might be time for Billie to go before Webber should see her, and it was the course of obvious prudence. But the C.I.D. had not engaged her to act prudently, but to obtain evidence that would break up the Mildew Gang. She said boldly: "He'll be startled to see me here. I think he arranged for me to be murdered before he came."

Boyle looked incredulous. "I don't see why he should do that."

"Well, he did.... I don't see why he should be telephoning from the next room."

Her eyes went to the instrument beside the bed of the sick man. She saw that she had roused suspicion in the mind of one from whose mind it could not be far. His answer had the tone of aiming to reassure himself rather than to convince her: "He wanted me to lie quiet.... He wouldn't have come if he hadn't...."

"He wasn't easy to persuade. But he couldn't resist the cheque. He didn't come till he'd locked me into a room, and telephoned for some men to deal with me—you can guess how."

"But you got here safely.... Do you know who the men were?"

"Guttins and Humphries, and a car-driver named Sinster. The police have got him and his car by now."

"Then, how did you get here?"

"I got this from Humphries' pocket while we were in the car, after Guttins had got out. It altered the conversation a lot."

Boyle stared at her, and at the weapon she had thought it might do no harm to show. He was evidently trying to visualize what had occurred, and to judge what its implications might be, without the clue which its elucidation required, and, at the same time, revising his opinion of her. "You seem," was all he said, "to be a very capable young woman."

"I don't know," she said, "but I got him here. You ought to thank me for that." It was a point which she wished to have in the front of his mind, if Webber should come in and say awkward things. He responded readily, though it was evident that the conversation was one of increasing difficulty to him.

"So I do. When I get about tomorrow, you'll find out how I feel. And you'll be able to help me more than I thought. But don't say anything to upset Webber now. We can't afford that tonight."

"No.... I can see that."

She might have said more, but Webber entered the room, and, as he did so, Boyle sank back, closing his eyes. She could not tell whether it were a case of genuine or simulated exhaustion. Perhaps something of both. She had noticed the increased effort with which his last words had been said.

Webber started visibly when he saw her standing there, the pistol still in her hand.

"How—?" he began foolishly, and checked his speech.

"You mean how did I get here?" she retorted, making her voice as amicable as she could, both to confuse him, and in deference to Boyle's suggestion that a quarrel should be avoided. "Mr. Guttins came and let me out, and then Sinster drove me here. Mr. Humphries let me have this. I believe it goes off at a touch."

Webber stared at her in a puzzled, malevolent silence. Suppose she really had made peace with the gang, or at least with Boyle, and those who were loyal to him? Suppose there were something here that he did not know, and that he had blundered in what he did? He was not satisfied with that explanation. He saw inconsistencies. But he could not get at the truth, and had learnt caution in such positions.

Guessing, more or less, what his bewilderment was, Billie added: "I don't know why you locked me in as you did. It was a silly thing to do; but it didn't really matter. Mr. Guttins soon let me out, and of course the important thing was for you to get here quickly. It didn't matter about me."

"We oughtn't to talk here. You'd better come into another room."

"I don't want to talk particularly. I think I'll stay with Mr. Boyle."

"I think not. If I am to be responsible for getting him well, I must have him left quiet."

"There won't be any noise from me."

"I must still ask you to leave the room. There are things which must be done."

"Of course, if you're staying with him— I only meant we needn't say any more about what's happened. It's best forgotten. And you ought to concentrate on getting Mr. Boyle well."

"I expect I shall be able to do that."

"I hope so, or it will be very awkward for you."

She left the room, putting the gun back into her bag, where it made a most awkward bulge, and was certainly doing no good to a fastening already strained. Her words had been meant at least as much for the sick man as for Webber, and she felt that she withdrew with the honours of war.

As she entered the lounge, she looked at the telephone in a hesitation which did not last more than a moment. The risk was too small, opportunity too good, not to be taken. It might be possible that she could be overheard on the bedroom instrument, but, even if that were so, it remained unlikely that the attempt would be made. She remembered that Boyle had not been attempting to listen in to Webber when she had come in, which he might be supposed to be willing to do. She remembered also that she had been able to hear the murmur of Webber's voice through the wall, though the words had been indistinguishable. Picking up the receiver, she asked quietly for the well-known number of Scotland Yard.

CHAPTER XIV.

BACKWASH TAKES A RISK

"I'M afraid," Superintendent Backwash said, "that I was a bit slow."

It was a generous admission from one who did not often allow that he had been wrong, nor very frequently have occasion to do so.

He had returned to Scotland Yard with Inspector Cauldron after learning that Billie had left Bright's Passage, with Sergeant Riddell and Doyle and Rogers upon her track, as it was here that he was likely to learn most quickly what had occurred; and he had just received Sergeant Riddell's report of how the car which they had pursued had evaded them in the Edgware Road.

Inspector Cauldron recognized the note of apology, but made no direct reply. His mind was concentrated upon the problem which it had become so urgent for them to solve. He said obviously: "It shows they weren't going back to the flat."

"Being in Edgware Road? Yes, evidently. Not making it their first call, anyway.... There's the point that she was going willingly. She may be equal to them yet, or a bit more. I've a lot of confidence in that young woman."

"We know she was willing when she got in. She may have seen reason to change her mind when it was too late. I don't see that she could do much when once she got in the hands of those poisoning thugs."

"Well, we must wait and see."

It was not an inspiring reply, but Superintendent Backwash had no better to make. He did not disguise from himself that the course of events might have been different had he been quicker to respond to Inspector Cauldron's restless anxiety when he had learned that Billie had entered the office suite in Bright's Passage, and remained there for so considerable a time. He had been influenced, perhaps to

76

the detriment of his own judgement, by the opinion that Inspector Cauldron fussed excessively concerning the safety of his new colleague, and he did not yet know how serious might be the result of his reluctance to intervene. Now he had given instructions for the most comprehensive search for the escaped vehicle possible to the extensive resources of the Metropolitan Police. There was nothing to do more but to wait for further reports to come in, unless they should raid the flat in Rivers Square. But what point would there be in that? On the knowledge they had, none. They knew that Billie was not there. They were having the flat watched. They knew that Boyle had not left.

They might question him. But was it likely that they would get any useful reply? He would say that Mrs. Risdon had called, and that she had left. It would be true, and held no imputation for him. The only result of the enquiry might be to alarm him in ways which would add to whatever Billie's dangers might be.

He knew—or thought he knew—the number of the car in which the kidnapping, if such it were, had occurred. For the moment, at least, they would be wiser to wait. Even Inspector Cauldron's impatience did not dispute that.... And then the telephone rang, and he heard Billie's voice on the wire.

"Yes. Superintendent Backwash. Can't you speak up a little? I can't hear very clearly."

"Please try. I don't want to be overheard."

He raised his head a moment to say: "Miss Wingrove's calling. You'd better listen in on the other line."

The next few minutes were silence, broken only by the superintendent's occasional: "Yes.... Yes, I can just hear you.... Yes, I'm listening; go on." Once—at Sir James Shorter's name—Cauldron gave a half-suppressed exclamation of astonishment, and at the conclusion of Billie's narrative the superintendent said briskly: "Now, Miss Wingrove, I understand that you've had to speak in a low voice, but I don't want any possibility of mistake. I understand you to say that someone called Sir James Shorter is accused by Boyle of having poisoned him at lunch today; that Boyle's certainly ill; that he's given Webber £5,000 to administer an antidote; that Webber is with him now in his flat at 17 Rivers Square; that you're alone in the next room; that, as far as you know, there's no one else in the flat except those two men and the housekeeper; that you were kidnapped by two other men named Guttins and Humphries, who are both loose somewhere in London now, and may be on your track; and that you captured the driver of the car, and have handed him and it over to one of our men who's on the way here. That right...? You're doing splendidly. Just carry on."

There was an exclamation of annoyance from the inspector as his superintendent hung up the receiver abruptly. "I didn't want the conversation," that gentleman explained, "to go on a second longer than was necessary. That was too dangerous for her. I didn't want to give any hint of what we may be going to do, even if I'd made up my own mind, which I can't say that I have, because there was no certainty that Boyle or Webber, or even the housekeeper, mightn't be listening in."

"She'd be likely to be needing help very soon, if they were doing that."

"She might—she might not. I suppose we shall have that driver brought in during the next few minutes. We ought to be able to get something useful from him."

"I don't suppose he'll know much."

"He won't have a list of the heads of the gang in his waistcoat pocket. But he'll know where he was driving to—and where they keep the car with the changeable plates, which is probably the same place. Oh, he ought to know quite a lot...! The trouble is we've not got enough time for all that ought to be done in the next hour. There's the Shorter angle, for one thing. We can't leave that, and we daren't risk a mistake."

"No. I can see that. It's not an easy thing to believe. Suppose they're using a faked name?"

"It's possible. But it doesn't sound likely. You'd better put someone on to find out where Shorter lunched, and who with. If I'm not sacked, I look like being promoted by this day next month, but it isn't easy to say which it's more likely to be. I reckon it's going to be a bigger risk than the Adam Street raid."

Inspector Cauldron did not dispute that, though he could only vaguely guess what the superintendent might be proposing to do. He knew that Shorter was not a man who could be lightly attacked. It was not merely that he was an archbishop's cousin, and a duke's probable heir, or even that he was an ex-Home Secretary, who had once been chief of their own department, so that the idea of prosecuting him had a flavour of impropriety. Beyond that, he was a man of high public character and popularity. Even apart from the suggestion of murder, an imputation that he was in any way associated with illegal traffic in noxious drugs would appear monstrous unless it could be fully sustained.

And it happened, unfortunately, that the Assistant Commissioner, to whose judgement the matter might appropriately have been submitted, was not in, as they had learned a few minutes before. But was "unfortunately" the right word? It was certain that Sir Henry would be cautious—perhaps overcautious—in what he did. And caution might not be the quality which the occasion required.

But Inspector Cauldron saw that the superintendent had gone to the heart of the problem when he had given instant instructions for enquiry to be made as to whether it were true that Shorter and Boyle had lunched together.

If they had, it did not prove that the accusation of poisoning was well founded. It might be no more than the suspicion of a sick and frightened man. But that suspicion was evidence that Boyle thought that Shorter might have a motive for taking his life, and would not be incapable of such a crime. It went far to demonstrate the nature of the probable relations between the two men, and of their joint activities.

On the other hand, if they had not lunched together, the basis of any accusation collapsed entirely.

The superintendent went on: "I'll stay here till the car comes in, and then decide what to do next. But you'd better get to the flat at once, and keep Webber there till you hear further from me. If any of the other beauties turn up, treat them in the same way. You can have any help that you need." He paused a second, and then had to raise his voice to arrest the attention of a man who was already half through the door. "You can do more than that. It's no use handling this thing with gloves. Tackle Webber. Frighten him, if you can. Get him to talk. Threaten him with arrest. Take any line you think well, and I'll back you up.

"As to Boyle, you'll have to act according to what condition he's in. But our line is to make them all understand that the game's up, and that their best chance is to give the others away. With rats like that you'll soon get some of them chattering, if they see that it's a chance of seeing more of the witness-box and a bit less of the dock.... All right; I've said enough. You'll know what to do."

As he concluded these hurried instructions he picked up the receiver of a telephone which had been ringing insistently for the twenty seconds they had occupied. "Miss Wingrove?" he said. "Put her through at once." He heard her say: "Is that Superintendent Backwash? I think you'd better—" The voice ceased. He raised his own to call Inspector Cauldron back. There was clearly something here that he ought to know. But it was too late. Inspector Cauldron had gone.... And the voice had ceased. In some way the connection had been severed, and it would be an act of doubtful wisdom to endeavour to reconnect, without certainty as to who might answer at Miss Wingrove's end of the wire.

He gave instructions that the telephone operator should be asked to make the connection instantly if Miss Wingrove should ring again; heard that Sinster and his car had come in, gave instructions that he should be charged with dangerous driving, using false number plates, and any other irregularities respecting the car which might be discovered, and held till he should have time to question him; enquired whether Chief Inspector Tolbooth were in, and, on being informed that he was, sent a message that he would be glad to see him.

"Sit down, Tolbooth," he said, as that astute officer entered the room; "I want to tell you one of the queerest tales that you ever heard, and to have your opinion of whether I am going to make myself a bigger fool than I have done yet."

CHAPTER XV.

WEBBER DOES IT AGAIN

BILLIE, sitting in the empty lounge after her uninterrupted conversation with Superintendent Backwash, had felt satisfied with the way that things were going, and moderately so of the security of her own position.

It was true that he had ended the conversation somewhat abruptly, without giving her assurance of support. She was doing "splendidly," and was to "just carry on." She may have expected some indication of more active support, but she recognized his caution for what it was. He had the facts now. If he felt that she would be able to handle the position there without interference from the police, she must suppose that he would be right. But his reticence did not necessarily mean that he would not be active to intervene.

She wished she knew with whom Webber had been talking on the phone. But he could not have mentioned her presence, of which, at the time, he had not been aware.

It would be more likely that it concerned Boyle than her. And even of him—was not the man here for the explicit purpose of saving his life, with £5,000 depending upon his being alive when the bank should open tomorrow?

And, putting the question of her own safety aside, had she not good reason to be content with the result of what she had done? She had uncovered the fact that Boyle and Shorter were associated in some way with the disposal of drugs, so that, when Boyle fell ill, it became natural for him to think that Shorter had used one of them for his destruction; and that they were both known to Webber, who obviously dealt in, and might actually import, these noxious poisons. She now knew, by sight and name, at least two subordinate members of the gang, besides the one whom she had obliged to drive himself to Scotland Yard.

It was an impressive list of successes, with the probability that it would result in the break-up of the gang. For was it likely, if Boyle should live, that he would not be willing to come to such terms with the police as would include the betrayal of the man who had practised against his life?

And if he should die, would there not be ground for investigations, if not of a resulting prosecution, such as would have the same effect in uprooting the whole evil organization, as a side-issue of what it did...? And meanwhile, for her further assurance, there was the pistol that bulged her bag.

It was in this mood of confidence that she heard the ringing of the bell of the outer door, and the steps of Mrs. Jepson along the passage. She waited in anticipation that someone would be shown into the room, making no motion beyond drawing her bag closer to her side, and opening it slightly, so that she could be quick to reach the weapon it held, and its existence would be hidden from others, unless she should rise from the ample depths of the armchair in which she was sitting.

But, after a short delay, the visitor was led past the lounge door to that of the bedroom beyond.

Billie recognized a man's footsteps following those of the housekeeper. She heard conversation as they passed her door. By what she heard—or rather did not hear, for the man's voice was lower than that of the woman—she made a correct guess that it was Guttins who was adding to the complication of her position now. But she told herself hopefully that he might not be thinking of her. It was doubtful that he would know that she had turned Humphries on to the pavement, or escaped from Sinster. He might still think that they had disposed of her, and have other matters of greater importance upon his mind. But she put aside a purpose which she had been forming to return to the bedroom and tell Boyle plainly, if he were in a condition to talk, who she was, and the purpose which had brought her there. She had done him a great service. If he now expected to live, he might be brought to see the expediency of coming to terms with the police, and betraying those who would have murdered him. But such plans must be deferred until Guttins should go. She felt sure that they would have no approval from him.

As she thought this, she heard the bedroom door open, and, next minute, Webber came in.

"Mrs. Risdon, "he said, with an emphasis on the false name, and a smile that she did not like, "I know more of what happened now than I did when I saw you before, though I don't know how you managed to get here. But I don't want anything to happen to you. I don't want to be mixed up in any violence at all. If you'll give me your word of honour that you won't tell the police about being locked in my office—or anything else that'll bring trouble to me—I'll let you out now, before Guttins knows you're here; and you'll be thanking me for saving your life when you thank me for that.

"I don't know that I shall thank you at all.... Do you mean that Guttins has told Mr. Boyle who he thinks I am?"

"He didn't say he thought. He was quite sure."

"And what did Mr. Boyle say?"

"He said he understood a lot now. He didn't say you were here."

"Well, I suppose Mr. Guttins won't stay all night."

"He may come in here any moment. If he does, you won't have long to live, I can tell you that. I know what their methods are."

Billie felt a cold tremor of fear at this warning. It was so obviously sincere. But she answered boldly: "He wouldn't do anything without Mr. Boyle's approval."

"And you think there'd be any help in that?" There was derision in the tone in which this question was asked, but Billie maintained her show of outward serenity as she replied: "I think Mr. Boyle has too much sense to make more trouble for himself here. And I don't think there would be much difficulty in walking out any time I want, without asking you. As a matter of fact, I'm intending to stay."

"Oh yes, there would. Mr. Guttins got Mrs. Jepson to lock the front door when he came in."

"Why did he do that, if he didn't know I'm here?"

"It wasn't about you. He's a gentleman who doesn't like to be disturbed unexpectedly."

"All the same, I shall leave any time I want." Her eyes fell, as she spoke, on the weapon he could not see. "And I'll tell you frankly I couldn't give the word of honour you ask for, even if I thought it worth doing. The police know already, and you've got far more reason to make friends with me than I have with you."

She saw the man change colour as she said this. She thought he was a coward with whom it should be easy to deal. So he was; but he was one whose wits did not cease to function because he feared. He said reasonably: "Well, I'm trying to save your life. You can't ask for anything much friendlier than that."

"Perhaps not. But I want something different. I want you to tell the police all you know about these men who are keeping on running the Mildew Gang."

"And how long should I live after I'd done that? I'm trying to save your life, and you're trying to get me to kill myself."

"Oh no, I'm not. With your help the police will arrest the lot so quickly they won't have time even to do themselves in—I think that's the right word—letting alone being any nuisance to you."

"I can't tell you what I don't know. I don't know about anything wrong, and I never did. But you'll remember, if you ever get out of here alive, that I did my best to get you to go."

"Well, I've no intention of doing anything of the kind."

"Then," he said, with an abrupt change of tone and manner, "you can't blame me if I look after myself."

As he spoke, his hand went to the key of the door beside which he had stood while this conversation proceeded. It was an instant's action to draw it out, step back through the door, and insert it on the outside. But Billie caught his intention as instantly, and sprang forward to prevent it.

"Oh no, you don't," she said sharply, and was pulling the door open again before he could turn the key. For a moment it moved indecisively, as they exerted increasing effort on either side. But his strength proved to be the greater. With a final wrench, he had it shut for the moment which was sufficient to turn the key.

Recognizing defeat, Billie went back to her chair. "It seems to be an absolute mania with the man to lock me into rooms," she thought angrily. "I wonder what good he thinks he's done himself now?"

But the more urgent question was not what good he had done himself, but what harm had he done to her? She saw that he might not believe that she had informed the police already, or might conclude that nothing could be proved against him if her mouth should be shut for ever.

"I'd better see," she thought, "what Superintendent Backwash has to say to this." With the same caution that she had used previously, she rang up Scotland Yard. The call was put through promptly, but after that there was some delay. It was not more than a couple of minutes, but it was decisive in its result. When she heard Superintendent Backwash's voice, she began: "I think you'd better know what's happening here. Guttins, the man I told you about before—" and stopped with the consciousness that she was talking on a dead wire. She tried to renew the connection, and realized that it was no longer operating. Mr. Webber's technique was not only repeating itself in its use of locks.

Not yet greatly alarmed, she thought: "He won't be long before doing something here. He must have heard me begin to speak." She considered that there were three men and a woman besides herself in the flat. She judged that there were few crimes, if any, that the men would not commit for the sake of their own skins, but the woman was another sort. Her presence would be an actual embarrassment to them in acts of violence of any criminal kind. Negatively, it was an advantage that she was there. And of the three men, one desperately ill, and another was evidently of those who prefer to remain in the background when differences are being settled on the physical plane. Of Guttins she was less sure, but she thought that, while they were all capable of murder to clear their paths, they were accustomed to delegate such crimes to others rather than commit them with their own hands. And there was the weapon beside her hand.... No, she told herself, she had little reason to fear.

Such were her thoughts, but they were not long ones, for she had little time to think of anything before the door was unlocked and Guttins entered. As she saw him she had the same difficulty in concealing her fear that she had experienced previously. It was not of anything that he appeared likely to do. It was the man himself who aroused an antipathy which was allied to terror. But it was a fear that she knew that she must not show.

She spoke with a forced lightness, hardly conscious of what she said: "It seems to be as much a habit for you to let me out as for Mr. Webber to lock me in. Is the man quite loony?"

"I haven't said I shall let you out, Miss Wingrove. What we do must depend on yourself. Mr. Boyle wishes to talk to you. But I agree that Webber's a fool."

"But perhaps you didn't know that I had this," she said boldly, lifting the revolver from the cushion at her side. "I certainly shan't stay a minute after I want to go."

Guttins looked at her and the gun she held without appearing particularly interested in it, or disturbed by what she said. His voice was still so quiet that it was barely audible as he replied indifferently: "You came here of your own will, Miss Wingrove, so I suppose this is where you wish to be. That was why I called Webber a fool. But I should be very careful with that gun, if I were you. If I'm right in recognizing it as one that our friend Humphries sometimes carries, you may have got it honestly or not—that's your matter—but you mayn't know that it goes off at the slightest touch. And if you start shooting unarmed men, and then try to say it was all a mistake, you may find that you've got yourself into an unpleasant position—very unpleasant indeed."

"You needn't worry about that. It would be a lot more so for the man who got the bullet," she replied cheerfully, while pointing the weapon somewhat more downward than before. "But I'm quite willing to see Mr. Boyle. I only left him because Mr. Webber said he needed medical attention."

As she spoke, she rose and followed Guttins into the adjoining bedroom.

CHAPTER XVI.

A QUESTION OF LIFE AND DEATH

THE Hon. Peter Boyle had been propped up with pillows. He looked more alive than when she had seen him half an hour before, though his eyes were heavy and his face of a leaden greyness. Webber was washing a syringe at the far side of the room, making it an easy guess that a second injection had been used to galvanize the nerves of the poisoned man.

The heavy eyes were turned upon Billie as she entered the room in a dull steady stare, which was not pleasant to meet. "So Mrs. Risdon and Miss Wingrove are the same person," he said slowly. "A nice fool you must have thought you were making of me."

"Most people change their names when they marry, don't they?" she replied, with an attempted lightness, and regretted it next moment, for she had determined that the truth was her strongest weapon, and her remark, however true in itself, was false in the implication that it conveyed.

"Most people," he echoed, "change their names when they're doing the work of a common spy.... Now, Miss Wingrove, we've got no time for any more nonsense. I want to know just what your game is, and what you thought you were doing here. And I want something more than that. I want you to tell me how we can be sure you'll do no more mischief if we let you go. We can take care of everything else, but I can't see any answer to that. And if you can—well, it will be a lot better for you."

There was a hard, menacing tone in the slow voice as he said this, which was not easy to meet with the confident smile which the position required, but she answered boldly: "I think I can tell you all you want to know, if not more. The only thing I couldn't tell you is how you'd take care of everything else if you could get rid of me. I should say you'd be in a bigger hole than you are now.

"All I've done has been meant to break up what I call the Mildew Gang, though, of course, that isn't the proper name to give it since Mr. Mildew got shot. I suppose you think it was a rather low thing to get to know you the way I did, but decent people think almost any means are justifiable to stop the kind of traffic that—"

"You'd better answer my question if you know how. I'm not going to listen to—"

"So I will.... You've got to remember, too, that I got Mr. Webber here, and probably saved your life, while I knew that my own was in danger every minute from you and your friends. I wonder why you think I did that."

"I might make a good guess. But you're not answering me. And we've no time to...."

"I'd give you answer enough if we were alone, but I might say some things you'd wish I hadn't when it would be too late, if I say them now."

She thought for a moment that she had made an effective answer. The hard, opaque eyes were fixed upon her with a deliberating stare. Was he considering whether her interest in him had been genuine? Whether she could be bought? Whether it might still be possible, and now worth his while, to marry her to secure her silence? He may have remembered that a wife cannot give evidence against her husband in English courts. He was a man to weigh chances coolly, and he must have seen that his position had become of a desperate difficulty, between the police enquiries which were approaching him so closely and the internal rivalries of the gang which had just come near ending his own existence.

She was confirmed in her satisfaction when the sick man, raising a hand with difficulty, motioned to the two other occupants of the room to withdraw. "You'd better leave us a few minutes," he said slowly. Guttins said: "All right, if you want," in his soft, barely audible way, and moved toward the door. To reach it he had to pass her side, and as he did so he struck her right elbow so sharply that the pistol which she had been holding downward fell to the ground. He stooped and picked it up during the next second, while she was only conscious of anger and of the sharp pain of the blow.

"It'll be safer with me," he said smoothly. "Lock the door, Webber; but stay here."

"Of course he'll do that," she said, laughing with a slight note of hysteria, for the pain was still acute, and anger was mixed with fear. "He's splendid at locking doors."

"It's no laughing matter for you," Guttins went on, with the deadly suavity which was so hard to meet without sign of fear;

"you've done too much harm already, and you're not going to do any more. What you'll tell us quickly is how you left the car, and where Humphries is now."

"I don't know where he is. He left it before I did."

"You'll have to be a lot plainer than that."

"I don't see why I should tell you anything."

"There's a very good reason. If you don't you'll either get a bullet where you won't like it, or an injection that'll make you go quietly to a place where we're less likely to be interrupted than we are here."

She looked round and saw that there was no help except in her own courage and her own wits. Webber had locked the door, as he was told, and dropped the key in his pocket. Boyle was watching the scene dumbly but, she thought, with apprehensive eyes. It was clear that Guttins was not taking orders from him, and the significance of that might concern him more closely than any question of what would happen to her.

As she did not answer at once, Guttins went on as quietly as before: "Webber, have you got anything with you of the right sort? Very well, then. Give her a shot if she won't talk.... If you scream or make any trouble," he added, turning to her, "I shall have the unpleasant duty of knocking you on the head with the weapon you were good enough to provide."

"I'm quite willing to talk," she answered, feeling that it was worth almost anything to gain time, and that there were things which it might be well for them to know. "Humphries left the car because he didn't want to be shot; and I found a way to persuade the driver to go on to Scotland Yard after he'd brought me here."

"Guttins"—the sick man spoke at last, with such authority in his voice as his condition allowed—"you're not going about this in the right way. You'd do better to leave it to me."

"I'm not leaving anything to you," Guttins answered smoothly. "I take my orders elsewhere now." The two men looked hard at each other, and Boyle met a sentence of death in the eyes that met his own. It was no more than he already knew when Guttins added, with the same quietness: "Webber's given you the last injection you'll get."

Billie spoke almost as quietly as he, but with an added courage, of which she was herself aware, her spirit rising in blended contempt and loathing of the callous villainy of the men before her. Boyle might be as vile as they, but it was not his crimes they condemned. He was to be left to die so that they might gain the favour of a new leader who had dropped the poison into his glass that noon. She said: "I think you're wrong about that. Mr. Webber will do the best he can to save Mr. Boyle's life. He'll go on with whatever he's been doing until now. He'll do it for £5,000; and because he'll be in the hands of the police if he doesn't, which will be very uncomfortable for him."

As she said it she was aware that the sick man was watching her in a changed way. She was his one hope once again, as she had been when she had set out to fetch Webber. It was pleasant in such a position as hers to feel that she had the support even of that impotent, ruthless man. And she felt that Webber also was of a divided mind. He might give way to Guttins' sinister and threatening influence. But, if he should do so, it would not be from inclination, but fear. And she was appealing at once to his fear and greed—probably the strongest passions that swayed his mind.

Guttins did not appear to be disturbed by her confident prediction of the conduct of the weaker man. He said, with no increase in his almost whispering voice: "Mr. Webber will do exactly what I say, and he'll begin with you. If there's any trouble, it won't matter much to you what he does afterwards."

Billie turned her eyes to an irresolute man. She was uncertain what he would do, but she recognized that Guttins might be his more immediate dread. She played her last card when she said confidently: "I quite understand that you'd half murder me if you dare, or perhaps quite. But you don't understand the position. The police are all round the flat. I expect they're at the door now."

And then, as though in response to her words, the doorbell rang.

CHAPTER XVII.

CAULDRON COMES ON THE SCENE

THE sound of the doorbell, coming as an echo of Billie's confident announcement, plainly startled Guttins. A look of apprehension came to his eyes, but it was quickly controlled. He said: "Webber, you'd better tell Mrs. Jepson to send any caller away. We don't want interruptions just now." But Webber stood hesitant, and Guttins—perhaps not being sufficiently sure of how he would act if he should leave the room—added: "No, perhaps better not. It isn't likely to be anything that matters to us."

He moved toward the door as he spoke, Humphries' gun in his hand. His watchful eyes were upon his companions within the room, rather than for anyone who might enter.

Mrs. Jepson had opened the outer door now, and a murmur of voices could be heard indistinctly. Billie recognized one that she knew. She said: "You'd all better make up your minds what line you're going to take. It's about the last minute you'll have."

Next moment Mrs. Jepson opened the door. "There's a detective officer waiting to see you, sir. I told him how unwell you are, but—"

Her agitated voice was interrupted by another behind her. "The lady quite properly did all she could to get me to go, but I had instructions not to do so without seeing you." Inspector Cauldron entered the room.

He glanced round at its four occupants in one comprehensive survey, observing particularly Guttins' position near to the door, and the weapon in his hand, at which he looked as he went on: "I think, in the first place, you'd better give me that gun."

There was a second's hesitation on the part of the man who held it, and who was thus called upon to decide his attitude to this police intrusion without time for thought. It must be surrender or defiance now, before he could tell what might be charged or intended against himself, or in what direction safety would lie. But his decision was quickly made. He passed over the revolver, with the remark: "I shall be very glad for you to take charge of it, Inspector. I had to take it from this young lady here, because she was holding it in a way that endangered our lives. She's the best one to tell you what right she has to it or why she was flourishing it round, but it wasn't a proper thing to have pointing all about in the room of a gentleman who seems to be rather seriously ill."

The explanation was plausible in tone and substance: the low voice confidential in tone. Inspector Cauldron dropped it into his pocket with no more reply than: "Well, it will be quite safe with me." He looked at Billie as he went on: "Perhaps you'd better tell me who these people are, and what you are all doing here."

She answered before any of the others attempted to speak: "Mr. Boyle is ill. He says that he has been poisoned at lunch today by Sir James Shorter. I fetched Mr. Webber to give him an antidote which he says no one else in this country has. That's Mr. Webber. Don't let him get away." (For Webber had been edging unobtrusively toward the door.) "This is Mr. Guttins you took the pistol from. I know nothing about him except that he tried to kidnap me in a car, and has just told Mr. Webber to drug me with an injection, and threatened to knock me on the head with the gun if I resisted."

"You charge him with those things?"

"Yes. I do. I should like you to arrest him now."

She looked toward Peter Boyle as she said this, expecting that it would have his approval, perhaps his gratitude, if not his more affirmative support. But she saw nothing to indicate such a feeling. Rather, she was conscious of an atmosphere of hostility that surrounded Cauldron and herself. These men might be engaged in deadly feud, they might be threatening each other's lives, but they desired no interference from the police; they would rely upon themselves for their defence at whatever extremity, rather than submit to the probing investigation of the law.

"You can arrest me if you like, Inspector," Guttins said coolly, "but I think you'll be sorry if you do. You'll find that what she's saying is partly imagination and partly lies. I came part of the way here with her in a car, and left her to finish the journey. If anyone tried to kidnap her, it's a bit hard to see how she got here; but, anyway, it was nothing to do with me. I didn't threaten her, or use any violence more than was necessary to take that gun away from her when it turned out that she had made Mr. Boyle's acquaintance here under a false name, and was asked to explain, which she seemed not to find it easy to do."

"Mr. Boyle," Billie retorted, looking toward the sick man, though with no more than a doubtful confidence, "can tell you that what happened was quite different from that."

But Boyle shook his head. He answered slowly, speaking with evident difficulty, but his words were distinct and clear: "I'd rather not be brought into this, Inspector. I don't want to charge the lady with anything. But I should say that what Mr. Guttins has told you is about right. I heard you call her Miss someone, and she's Mrs. Risdon to me. It's a bit unusual for an unmarried woman to be wearing a wedding ring. But I don't make any charge. Whatever her game is, she's done no good for herself here.... But I'm not well. I expect you can see that. I should be very glad if you'd leave me quiet. Mr. Guttins didn't do anything more than was necessary for our own safety. I'm sure Mr. Webber'll tell you the same."

Webber answered with real or assumed reluctance, as though not willing to be drawn into a matter which did not concern him, but constrained to admit the truth. "Yes. It's no matter of mine. But that was about it."

Billie was in no doubt as to whether Inspector Cauldron would believe her version of what had occurred, but she saw that it might be possible to put a different construction upon it, if the three men were prepared to swear to the same tale. She could not tell how far it might seem to him to obstruct the charge she had made, or what course he would take. Nor did he indicate what he thought, as he replied to the sick man with a courtesy due rather to his position than to himself: "Yes, sir. I'll see you don't get any more disturbance here.... I'll have a few words with you privately, Mr. Guttins, if you'll step out with me."

Inspector Cauldron led the way from the room, and Guttins followed hesitantly. A few minutes later they could be heard leaving the flat together.

"I don't think he'll trouble you any more, Mr. Webber," Billie said. "You'd better go on doing what you can to earn that £5,000."

Webber looked at her venomously. He was a frightened man. For many years greed had made him a criminal, and caution had kept him in the discreet backwaters of crime. Now, through no indiscretion with which he could blame himself, he was uncomfortably close to the investigating activities of the law, and in danger of its penalties for things he had, and perhaps for some that he had not, done.

Nor was the law his only, or even his sharpest, fear. He was being pressed to do that which he knew Sir James Shorter would not forgive. And he knew enough of what had happened to another man who had incurred Shorter's displeasure to be terrified at the thought. Besides that, he saw that he had been cajoled or bribed into acting in a way that provided strong evidence that he had accepted the tale that Boyle had been poisoned, and that he knew the nature of the poison used. That might land him in the witness-box, or even the dock. He had a shrewd fear that the road from the one to the other might not be long.

And for all these troubles he blamed the girl who was advising him now. The bitter hatred of a cowardly and cornered man was in his eyes as he answered: "If some women had their necks wrung, it would be a quieter world for decent people to live in."

"That's an idea," Billie agreed, with a lightness which reflected her relief since Inspector Cauldron had appeared. "And I can tell you of another that's quite as good. The law doesn't exactly wring necks, but it does something else to them which does just as well. The necks of people who poison others, like Sir James Shorter, and—don't you think complicity's rather a good word?"

"I've told you all along that I don't know what you're talking about. I don't believe anyone's poisoned anyone. Nor—"

"And that's why you came here, with the antidote for a strange poison you never supplied to anyone, and know nothing about? The law may be an ass, but you'll find you've got a hard job to make it believe that...Mr. Webber," she continued, changing to a more serious tone, "You can say anything you like about me, and tell Inspector Cauldron any lies you please. As he wouldn't believe them, it really makes no difference at all. But if you want to save your own skin—I won't say anything more about the £5,000—you'll do all you can to get Mr. Boyle well. You needn't be afraid of anything Sir James Shorter can do, if you manage that. I expect he'll have other things to think of by this time tomorrow, even if Mr. Boyle wouldn't be able to take care of him."

It was hard to judge what effect this advice had Webber continued to stand irresolutely, as one who could not make his choice between different fears; and Boyle, who had been listening with a puzzled expression in eyes which were again showing the torpor which recurred as the effect of the antidote lessened, interposed with: "Miss Wingrove, I wonder why you're so anxious that Webber should save me. It doesn't seem very consistent with some things you've been doing lately."

"No," Billie answered, speaking perhaps the first sincere words he had heard from her, "I suppose it does seem rather loony to you. But can't you understand that anyone may want to do all they can to break up a gang of drug traffickers, and still not want to see one of them die of poison if he can have help?"

"I didn't say anything about drug traffickers."

"No, but I did."

"I cannot allow you to connect my name with anything of the kind."

"What's the use of talking like that, when it's as plain as—?"

"Just this, that it will be no use for you to make assertions that everyone will deny. Whatever I said to you about Shorter, or anything else, wasn't meant for the police, and it will be no use repeating it to them. I shall say you invented the whole thing—that you probably made up a tale for which you thought they'd pay you—and anyone else who knows Shorter would see that it's absurd. But if you're wise enough to know when the game's up, you might find that it wouldn't be long before a thousand pounds in untraceable one-pound notes would be lying somewhere where they could be picked up—"

"I dare say they would. But they're not for me. Hadn't you better see about persuading Webber to do what he can for you before you get worse?"

"It's not time for the next injection. Not for half an hour yet. I've no doubt that he'll give it me when it's due."

"Well, if you're sure!" She looked doubtfully at the sullen, hesitant man of whom they spoke, whose doubts had actually been increased by the words which had just been spoken. For if Boyle were confident that they could out-bluff or out-swear any witnesses the police could muster, there was nothing to fear from them, and the fear of Shorter remained. He considered that Guttins had already regarded him as the one on whose side it would be the more advantageous to be. He thought there was warning in that, for he had a high opinion of the. cunning of that quiet-mannered man. He was very near to a decision to walk out of the flat, and leave Boyle to the operation of the still deadly drug, even though it should involve the loss of £5,000, when Inspector Cauldron re-entered the room.

In the interval he had sent Guttins, with a sufficient escort, to Scotland Yard, stirring thereby that surprised individual to raise his voice in protest, and reveal that it squeaked uncontrollably in its higher tones; and he had made a telephone report to Superintendent Backwash, and received further information and instructions from him.

He came in briskly, prepared for further action, and addressed Boyle at once: "Mr. Boyle, you'll be glad to hear that we are taking immediate action against Sir James Shorter. He may be already under examination at Scotland Yard. We shall detain him there while we take a statement from you, and collect the other evidence that the case requires, so we shall have to move quickly. I suppose you know that our powers of detention are very limited till a charge is made."

A man in Boyle's physical condition is unlikely to be as quick and subtle of wit as when in control of his faculties, and that may be his excuse for the look of satisfaction which stirred the dullness of his eyes on hearing that Sir James Shorter was not having a happy time. But that was for no more than a transient moment. Then he said: "There must be a mistake somewhere. I don't know what you think this has to do with me."

"We have information that Shorter poisoned you when you lunched with him today, which explains the condition you are now in."

"Who told you that nonsense?"

"It is your own statement to Miss Wingrove."

"It is nothing of the sort. I'm afraid Miss Wingrove has an extraordinary imagination. She isn't always sure about her surname."

"It's no use talking like that," Billie interposed. "What about that £5,000 cheque you've given Mr. Webber to get you well?"

"I don't know how much you misunderstand, or how much you invent, *Mrs. Risdon*," the sick man replied. "You don't seem to be very clear about your own name. But I'm under no obligation to discuss my financial affairs with you, or with the inspector, for that matter. All I want is that you'll be good enough to let me alone."

He spoke with increasing slowness and apparent difficulty as he concluded this sentence, at the end of which he closed his eyes, as though exhausted by the effort he had made.

Inspector Cauldron looked at him speculatively. His attitude was not unanticipated. It was the biggest risk that Superintendent Backwash had taken in moving against Shorter. Without Boyle, and if the other members of the gang who were now identified took the same attitude, what had they to go upon but Billie's evidence, and some supporting facts of which different explanations might be possible? But he had one line of attack on which he relied. He said: "Well, Mr. Webber, I should like your account of what brought you here."

Webber blinked at him uneasily. He had the look of a trapped animal. The fact was that he had concocted some fairly plausible explanations, but he saw that they would collapse, and convict himself, if others, questioned separately, should tell different tales.

It was a position in which previous knowledge of the line which Boyle would take or approve was desirable, and consultation with

Guttins was even more necessary. "I came here," he said, "on Mr. Boyle's invitation. I don't see that any explanation's needed beyond that."

"But I do. Miss Wingrove told you that Mr. Boyle had been poisoned. She didn't give you the name of the poison. How did you know what the right antidote would be?"

"I haven't said that I did."

"No? It was a strange thing that you should, unless you knew who'd given the poison, and what it was. I wonder whether you realise the serious position that you are in unless you can give some better explanations than you have yet."

"I haven't tried to explain anything. I don't agree that you've got the facts right. Anyway, if you threaten me I'd rather have my solicitor present before I say anything more."

"I'm not threatening you. I'm giving you a warning for your own good. But you've a right to refuse to answer questions. Does that refusal also apply to why you locked Miss Wingrove in your office, because if it does I—"

"I locked her up because I thought she wasn't right in her head."

"Why should you think that?"

"Because she told me such a queer tale. I didn't believe it, but I thought I ought to find out, and secure her meanwhile. But she wasn't locked up long. I arranged for Mr. Guttins to look after her, and let her come here if he thought it the best thing to do."

"Did you find that what she'd told you was true?"

"I don't know about that. Some of it certainly wasn't."

"What wasn't?"

Webber's replies had become slower and slower. The pressure of their questions plainly embarrassed him, without giving him cause or confidence to refuse any reply. But now he became silent.

"You'd rather not answer that?" Inspector Cauldron continued sharply. "Miss Wingrove wasn't wrong when she told you that Mr. Boyle had been poisoned, was she?"

Webber glanced towards the bed, as though seeking orders or instructions, from that direction. He got nothing, for Boyle lay with his eyes closed, as though unconscious of what was being said, but it may have brought the fact to his mind that Boyle had made it plain that he did not wish to make Shorter's action a matter for the police to deal with. Clearly, he intended to deny, and would wish others to deny it to them.

"I certainly have no reason to think that Mr. Boyle has been poisoned," he answered. "It always seemed to me to be a most improbable tale."

"I'm glad to hear you say that, because you've got to come with me to Scotland Yard, and Miss Wingrove had the idea that it was important that you should be administering some antidote during the night."

He watched Webber keenly as he said this, for it was the trump card on which he relied, and, for a moment, he doubted that it would prove a winner.

Webber certainly did not look pleased at the idea of visiting the head-quarters of the C.I.D. He said: "I don't know why you want me to go there, or that you've got any right to ask. I suppose it's no use saying I won't come; but it's under protest, if I do, and I warn you that you'll hear nothing more from me till I've got a good lawyer present, to see that you don't put something on to me that I haven't said."

Actually, he was not entirely displeased. He had seen quickly, in a cunning mind, that if Boyle should recover he could not blame him for not continuing his ministrations after he had been forced to leave; if Boyle should die, he might persuade Shorter that he had never intended to save him; and if there should be a Prosecution of Shorter following Boyle's death, he would be in the position of having been prevented by the police from saving the life of the poisoned man. That, he thought, might be very awkward for them! Could he not say that, though he had not credited the tale of the poisoning, he had still been taking action which would have saved Boyle's life if it were true? Looking ahead, the ugly rail of the dock faded, and that of the witness-box became a more welcome vision. He saw more than one basis for making terms with the police. He would escape, as he had done years before. Narrowly, perhaps, but still escape.... No, he had no objection to going.

But Boyle, who had heard all, looked at it differently. With more animation of manner than had appeared possible a few minutes before, he opened his eyes, and even raised his head stiffly for a few inches to say: "You mustn't take Webber away. It's essential he stays with me."

Inspector Cauldron replied in the deferential tone he had used to him before: "Well, sir, if it's all a mistake about this poisoning tale, you can't need him here, even if he is the only man who knows all about it, and what the antidote is. You can't need him more urgently than we happen to do, and I'm afraid our business comes first.... What I think I'll do is to telephone to your own doctor, if you'll tell me his name. He's sure to be a good man, and he'll know best what you've got wrong."

"I don't need any doctor. I need Webber. Surely tomorrow'll do for you? It's getting late now."

"If you'll tell me that you've been poisoned by Sir James Shorter, and how you know that Webber has the antidote for whatever he gave you, I'm willing to listen, but if not I don't see any reason why I shouldn't take him along."

"If I've not been poisoned, I don't see what you want with Webber, and if I have he ought to stay here. That sounds better sense to me."

Inspector Cauldron was aware of the logical weakness of his position, and had the reply ready: "He won't be charged with that. It's the locking up of Miss Wingrove and the subsequent attempt at kidnapping of her by his friends that he's got to explain.... I'm afraid, Mr. Webber, you'll have to come along with me."

Boyle gave a gesture of resignation. "You win," he said, with a returning exhaustion; now that the battle of wits was over. "Let him stay, and you shall have the whole tale, and make the most of it that you can."

Inspector Cauldron took out his notebook, but Boyle went on: "But you must let him give me something first. It's past the time: I can't feel that I've got any use of my legs now.

It was not a request that could be refused. "Very well," he said. "And, Miss Wingrove, you might go into the next room and telephone the superintendent why I'm detained here."

CHAPTER XVIII.

THE INDIGNATION OF SIR JAMES SHORTER

SUPERINTENDENT BACKWASH, having learnt that the Hon. Peter Boyle and Sir James Shorter had lunched together at Boyle's invitation, and in a private room, so that their conversation had not been liable to overhearing except when the waiter had been in, had decided upon the abrupt action in which, he felt, lay the best, if not the only, hope of finally destroying the Mildew Gang. And in doing this he knew that it would not be a case of "victory or Westminster Abbey" for him. It would be promotion or disgrace, which is a far less satisfactory programme. To arrest a man of the standing of Sir James Shorter on a charge which could not be sustained, and to do this with an impetuosity which allowed no time for obtaining the approval of his superiors, was not an action which would be condoned. It could be justified by success, but by nothing less decisive than that.

But he knew that, more than once before, a policy of caution had been pursued, with failure for its result. He knew that it was his slowness to act on which, added to their own astuteness, the wealthy and well-reputed individuals who controlled the gang largely relied. He had proved what can be done by prompt and resolute action on the occasion of the Adam Street fire,[1] and that success may have encouraged him to a further audacity, which seemed to deny his long-established character for cautious and conventional methods.

But the details of his course of action were still consistent with the solidity of his reputation. He did not commit the gaucherie of sending an officer to arrest the eminent but suspected man. He telephoned to his home, and was informed by his secretary that he was at dinner. He said that he was sorry to trouble Sir James, but he would be glad if he could make it convenient to call at Scotland

---

[1] See *The Return of the Mildew Gang*.

Yard during the next hour. It was a matter of urgency. The secretary said he would give the message to Sir James. He returned to say that it would not be convenient, as Sir James had guests. Perhaps the superintendent could make it convenient to come to him? The superintendent regretted that this would not be possible, and the secretary asked: Could he tell Sir James what the nature of the business was? No; it could not be stated on the telephone. The secretary went to obtain Sir James's instructions again.

He returned to ask how long the business was expected to take. Would half an hour be enough? The superintendent replied, with doubtful veracity, that it should be more than sufficient. The secretary said that Sir James would come. He had instructions to order the car now. In less than a quarter of an hour Sir James was shown in.

He was a large, rather awkwardly built man, with black, greying hair, rather pompous in manner, though less so in words. He was not grossly fat, nor had he any appearance of dissipation. But it would be judged that he drank enough, if not more. He was not regarded by his friends as a stupid man. They would even seek his advice. But most of them would have called him heavy, if not dull. Yet they would have allowed that his snooker was good and his bridge sound.

His period as Home Secretary had been without any awkward incident, to which that office is peculiarly liable, so that it has done more harm than good to the reputations of most of those who have occupied it. He was not brilliant in oratory. But he had an undeniable public popularity, which may have been partly derived from that of the great family to which he belonged.

Superintendent Backwash rose as he entered, and moved a chair into position for him to occupy. It avoided any question of shaking hands, a familiarity which, in fact, Sir James would not have approved.

He commenced while still standing: "I understand, Superintendent, that there is a matter of some urgency requiring my attention here. If you will be good enough to—"

"If you will be good enough to sit down, Sir James? It is a matter of gravity which has come to our notice during the last four hours. You may have heard of a man named Guttins?"

Superintendent Backwash watched closely for any symptom of surprise or alarm which might be roused by this harmless question, but there was none to observe.

Sir James, lowering himself into a chair which creaked somewhat under his weight, answered indifferently:

"Guttins? No, I can't say that I have. Not to remember. It's a rather unusual name, isn't it? Perhaps, if you gave me a few particulars—"

"He's a man we have arrested this afternoon. He's on his way here now. We expect a statement from him of very particular interest."

"About what?"

"About some drug-traffickers who have come to be known here as the Mildew Gang."

"Mildew? That's another unusual name. There was Cornelius, who shot himself a few weeks ago. A very pleasant companion at the card-table. I seldom remember being more surprised. But of course that couldn't have been the same man."

"He didn't shoot himself. Peter Boyle shot him."

"*Peter Boyle?* It sounds incredible! But, of course, if you have evidence—"

"We have known it from the first. It was just the legal evidence that we lacked. But killing each other—"

At this point most inopportunely, they were interrupted by the telephone bell. The superintendent, who had given instructions that no calls were to be put through for the next half-hour except on the Mildew matter, took up the receiver in an anticipation that was more than realized. He heard Billie's voice informing him at some length, which he did not attempt to curtail, of the conversation in which she had taken part in the adjoining bedroom, and finally of Boyle's agreement to talk on condition that Webber should continue his ministrations.

It was just what he required to give him confidence for the interview which was beginning.

"I have had," he said, "important confirmation of the extraordinary story which had reached us from other channels. Boyle has decided to talk. His statement is being taken now."

"You mean he admits having shot Mildew?"

"I can't say whether his statement will cover that ground. It is the matter of his own poisoning with which, at the moment, we are primarily concerned."

"You say Boyle has been poisoned? It must have happened during the last few hours. I can tell you he was all right at midday. In fact, I saw him eat as good a lunch as any man need wish to have."

"So I understood."

"If you have troubled me to come here, Backwash, because you heard that, I must tell you that I think you should have used the telephone. I could have let you know in three minutes that, apart from the fact that I met Boyle at lunch, when he seemed perfectly normal, and was certainly in good health, I know nothing that can be of any assistance to you. Nothing at all."

"I'm afraid I can't agree there. You could tell me, for instance, what business you had with him today, and how the appointment was made."

"So I could, of course, if it appeared that it could have any possible connection with whatever may have occurred since. Actually, it could have none. But this also could have been dealt with on the telephone, without troubling me to come here."

"Perhaps I could judge of that better if you would kindly answer my question."

For the first time, Sir James showed an uncontrolled annoyance. "I think," he said, with a stiffening of his previous formality, "that you must leave me to judge of that. Of course, should you tell me anything which would cause me to alter my opinion—but it is practically impossible.... Is Sir Henry in?"

"No. He is out of town till tomorrow afternoon."

"So I should suppose. When he returns, kindly tell him that I shall always be pleased to give him any help in my power, and ask him to kindly ring me up if that can apply to this Boyle affair, of which, so far, you have told me practically nothing."

With these words, Sir James got up to go, and Superintendent Backwash saw that the moment of decision had come.

To let him go—to lay the facts before those on whom the responsibility for ultimate decision naturally lay—such were the dictates of prudence, and the traditions in which he had been trained were urgent in their support. But to do so was, in his opinion, to throw away the best—perhaps the only—opportunity of breaking up the Mildew Gang and convicting its principals which his department was ever likely to have. That was, of course, on the assumption that Sir James was a guilty man.

If he were wrong—if Sir James were innocent—then he must look upon his career as irretrievably damaged, if not ended. But if Boyle's accusation were true—if he had struck at Boyle as Boyle had certainly struck at Mildew, with the dual aims of removing a man who, having become suspect himself, had become dangerous to his associates, and of acquiring entire control of the huge funds of the gang—then the one chance was to prevent him communicating with his subordinates. With Boyle confessing, and Shorter removed from any possibility of further control, those men would be left running round like a fowl that had lost its head. Those were the conditions from which panic came. Where, for some previous exasperating years, it had only been possible to convict men who would not say—who perhaps even did not know—who their principals were, there would he the hope of commencing from the top, and ending with a full net.

"I am sorry, Sir James," he said, with a more distantly official voice than he had used previously, and some inward annoyance that it was hardly as firm in quality as he would have liked it to be, "but if you refuse to answer my question I'm afraid I must detain you until further enquiries have been completed."

If the stare of incredulous astonishment with which Sir James received this intimation were not genuine, he was an actor of exceptional ability lost to the stage.

"Backwash," he said, "you have had the reputation of being a sound man. If you go on like this I shall think you are qualifying for a mental home."

"Perhaps I am. But you know yourself, Sir James, that, in a matter of this kind, we have to examine every possibility, however unlikely; and the question I asked is a very natural one, in view of the fact that you lunched with a man who afterwards became seriously ill, and who has almost certainly been poisoned."

"What makes you so sure of that?"

"Statements made by Boyle and others."

"Yes, of course. But what are they? And have you no medical report? I must say, Superintendent, that you are not treating me with a reasonable frankness, and if there *were* any direction in which I could help you it would not be improved by that attitude."

"If you had treated my first question in a different manner—but I think, before going further, I ought to tell you that you are accused—not by us—of poisoning Peter Boyle with intent to murder."

"Who is the author of that absurdity?"

"Boyle himself, and his evidence is confirmed by others. Particularly by the man who is said to have supplied the drug, and is now administering the antidote. I need scarcely say that such an allegation against a gentleman of your position and character is not lightly accepted here; but the evidence is sufficiently circumstantial to make me doubtful whether I should continue this conversation without giving the customary warning."

"You mean the 'used in evidence' gag? You needn't trouble about that, Backwash. I know the ropes. And now you've been a bit franker with me than you were before, I'll tell you what I can about my meeting with Boyle today."

"I am sure it is the wiser course."

"Well, there's not much to tell. I met him at his invitation, not mine. We are acquaintances; you could scarcely put it higher than that. I was rather surprised to be asked, and more so when I found he had engaged a private room. I suppose I need scarcely say that I didn't provide anything, either food or liquor. It was an *à la carte* meal. We ordered differently. I might think out what he had, if it should be important to know.

"We didn't talk any business, nor anything of a private nature, so that I was more puzzled than before as to why I was there. I thought he might have some proposal to make that wasn't easy to begin on, and I offered to take him on to the club in my car, and perhaps cut in at a game of bridge, but he said he had an appointment with a lady he couldn't break."

Superintendent Backwash listened to this statement, and found nothing in it to encourage him in the course he had decided to take. The one item that he could check—the appointment—was true. There was nothing in that. Boyle had doubtless mentioned it, and Shorter guessed that it would have come to the knowledge of the police. If so, he was trying to buy belief in the other details he gave at a very cheap rate. But while the superintendent hesitated, Sir James spoke again: "I'm not pressing you to give me particulars of the allegations which have been made, though I think you should, for your own protection rather than mine. But I noticed one word you used. You said that these allegations are 'circumstantial.' I should like to remark that false accusations usually are, and it is by a close examination of that often needless embroidery that their quality is disclosed."

Superintendent Backwash knew this to be true. He knew equally that it is by the needlessly circumstantial explanations of guilty men that their veracity is most often discredited. But Sir James seemed to be little addicted to this treacherous verbosity. Being warned now, he would be on his guard, with the advantages of his exceptional experience, and probably exhibiting an attitude which had been often rehearsed in his mind before. That is, if he were guilty. There was always that disconcerting doubt. For there was none that Sir James understood how to act an innocent part. He did not even show any great curiosity as to the details of the allegations, or the men who made them. Yet even that aloofness had not been overdone. He had spoken a warning as to the inexpediency of withholding them, and left it at that.

The superintendent had a belated doubt as to whether it might not have been better to approach Sir James in a different manner. Would he have talked more freely then, and made the one fatal slip which the guilty man is so likely to do? Perhaps. But there was still the objection that it would have been necessary to leave him free to give orders for the false witness of those on whom he could depend, and perhaps for the violent removal of others who would be essential to the police.

It was true that nothing in Sir James's public or private record indicated him to be a man of such ruthless criminality. It was probably those records on which he would rely, and which would be his strongest defence. But there was no less repellent possibility. No man with any tolerable standards of decency could have become the trusted intimate of Peter Boyle in controlling the international drug-distribution of the Mildew Gang.

"I have no doubt you are right," he added, after a rather long pause, pregnant with final decision, "and you can depend upon every statement we may receive being most carefully weighed, with that possibility before us.... I am sorry that I must ask you to remain here, at least until those of Boyle and Webber have been fully considered, or until Sir Henry's return."

Shorter rose from his chair, his face flushing darkly. "You can't really mean—?" he began. "You first threaten me in an outrageous manner unless I give you some absolutely useless details about to-day's lunch, and then when I have done it—" He checked himself with an obvious effort for self-control. "Backwash," he said, "I know you have the power to do this, and I'm not such a fool as to attempt to resist the law. But you've yourself to consider as well as me. With my position, this will be all over England—I might almost say all over the world—tomorrow. And if you're making a terrible mistake, as you most certainly are—" He checked his voice, which had gradually risen again, and added in a quick, persuasive tone: "You feel you have your duty to do. I appreciate that. But have you thought that this thing may have been expressly arranged so that suspicion would be directed upon myself? I don't profess to understand how or way that should be done. That's more than anyone could expect. But when I think of that purposeless lunch appointment—there's something here that requires probing, and I ought to be on it as well as you."

"It's a possibility," the superintendent conceded readily, for it was actually one to which he had given some consideration, and it still lurked uneasily at the back of his mind. "I can understand that anyone who wished to poison Boyle might be glad to throw suspicion on you. But it doesn't fit all the facts—not so far as we've got them yet. Boyle didn't make arrangements for his own poisoning, and he'd no adequate object for accusing the wrong man. Still, we'll watch that.... But what you're trying to make me feel is that I'm not acting fairly to a man of your character, and in your position, and not fairly to myself because, if I am shown to be wrong tomorrow, I shan't be likely to get any support even from my own chiefs.

"I see all that well enough, but I'll tell you plainly, I'm not thinking first of myself for you. I'm thinking of all the evil this drug-trafficking does, and I'd rather risk some annoyance for an innocent man, or my own career, than make a mistake of the other kind."

"But what mistake can you make? A man in my position doesn't vanish because of a crazy, incredible accusation of this kind. I've too much to lose. And, for that matter, I shouldn't know how to begin. You can have my passport, if you like. You can put your best men round the door. I'm willing to give you my word of honour that I'll report here daily, if you want that.... Surely that will be enough—at least, till you get in touch with Sir Henry again?"

"I'm sorry, Sir James. But we wanted Mildew, and Boyle shot him just as the warrant was ready. We wanted Boyle, and were on his track, and he gets poisoned just as the net's being drawn in. You can see what my position is."

Sir James saw that protest would not avail. He became stiffly formal again. "Well, I've warned you, and I think you'll live to regret what you're doing now. I suppose you won't object to my ringing up Forsyth and Jones? I can have my solicitors here?"

"You shall have every facility for that purpose," the superintendent replied in a manner which had become as officially distant, though less stiffly so than that of the ex-Home Secretary. He had staked everything on the assumption that Sir James was a guilty man, and on that premise he must rely. He picked up his office phone to give instructions that Sir James was to be lodged in such comfort as Scotland Yard provides for those of its involuntary guests as are not formally charged, and as he did so the instrument on the other side of his desk commenced its insistent call. He transferred his attention to it to hear Billie's voice: "Yes. I'm still at Rivers Square. So's Inspector Cauldron. He wants you to come here at once. We're in rather a jam."

"What kind of a jam?"

"Well, Mr. Boyle wouldn't say anything till he'd had an injection, and, so far, we haven't persuaded Mr. Webber to give it. He wants a promise first that Inspector Cauldron's unable to give."

"And you think I could?"

"No. I don't. But you might think of something that we can't. Mr. Boyle looks nearly dead now."

"I'll be with you in fifteen minutes, if not less. You'd better go on trying all the means you know. I'll get a couple of good doctors to come along too."

He had been silenced in much that he might have asked by the fact that Sir James was still in the room. But he knew himself to be on the edge of a pit the depth of which was easy but not pleasant to see. If Boyle should die without making the statement on which he relied—if Webber should deny the most vital facts—where would he be then?

He turned to Sir James to say: "I'm sorry to hear that Boyle has taken a turn for the worse. But we must still hope that it will be possible to pull him through." He hoped that he had overheard nothing which that explanation would not be sufficient to cover.

CHAPTER XIX.

WEBBER MAKES CONDITIONS

THE trouble had already started before Billie had finished telephoning Superintendent Backwash the good news that Boyle had promised to talk. His one condition, that he should first have another of the life-giving injections, of which he was in evident need, had been reasonable in itself, and had not appeared to involve difficulty or appreciable delay. A hypodermic syringe is soon used. Webber was there for the explicit purpose of using it.

But Webber had a condition to stipulate which appeared reasonable to him. He said that, before he would do anything more, he required a plainly worded pledge that he should not be involved in any criminal proceedings which might follow from the statement which Boyle had promised to make.

"You know I can't promise that," Inspector Cauldron replied, "when I don't even know what Mr. Boyle may be going to say. I haven't the authority, to begin with. I doubt whether anyone less than the Home Secretary has, and he might find it to be one that he couldn't keep.... But I'll promise that, if you do all you can for Mr. Boyle now, we'll do all we can to make it easy for you. You can't ask for more than that."

"I'm not asking for anything. I don't want anything to do with the thing at all."

"You can't help that now. You're in it up to the neck. All I'm asking you to do is to help to get yourself out."

"That's just where we differ."

"And the way you're behaving is just accusing yourself."

"I don't see that either."

"You wouldn't make this difficulty if you weren't afraid of what Mr. Boyle may be going to say."

"That's different."

"The difference isn't easy to see."

"Of course it is. I might be accused of things I've never even thought of doing."

"Such as supplying a poisonous drug, with a criminal purpose, when you had meant it for something else?"

"Well, suppose it were that."

"Then, if you were innocent, you'd have very little to fear. English law requires proof. You know that. Suspicion isn't enough."

"You mean, if I were tried, I should get an acquittal more likely than not?"

"Without proof, I should call it a sure thing."

"And who'd pay the bill?"

It was a question to which Inspector Cauldron had no satisfactory answer to give. It is one of the worst abuses of English criminal law that a person falsely accused may recover the outlay incurred in his defence if he be prosecuted by another private citizen, but not if the prosecution be in the name of the Crown. It is a vicious application of the theory, indefensible in itself, that the Crown can do nothing wrong. Webber's question was one that might occur to many when faced by the official attitude that an accused man, if confident of his ultimate acquittal, has nothing about which to worry, and Webber had been under the shadow of criminal procedure once before. The thought came more promptly and insistently to him than it might to most, he being a miserly man.

"I don't know about that. But I know you'll be in Queer Street if you let a man die while you've got the means of saving his life in your own hands."

"But you don't know that I have."

"I know why you came here."

"Do you? I came to find out what the truth was. I told Miss Wingrove I didn't believe her tale. It sounded nonsense, and that's what I think it was. But I didn't know she was a police agent, or I shouldn't have come a step here; and you'll either give me the promise I ask, or you'll get nothing more from me."

So the wrangle went on its abortive course, followed with silent intentness by the man who lay waiting for its result, and who had such urgent cause, perhaps for the first time in his life, to wish that the force of Jaw might be of prevailing strength, until Billie returned from her prolonged conversation with Superintendent Backwash.

Inspector Cauldron explained the deadlock. "Perhaps," he said, "you can make him see that it's better for himself to try to help the police, and try to save a man's life at the same time, than to let him die just to be a nuisance to us."

"I've told Mr. Webber before," she answered cheerfully, "that he seems determined to get hanged, if there's any possible way in which he can manage it, and now he seems to have found a fresh chance."

Webber heard this with angry and sulky eyes, but he did not appear to be frightened by the warning it was intended to give.

"I've done nothing wrong yet," he answered stubbornly, "and I'm doing nothing wrong now. I'm not a doctor. If I have got something like you think, I needn't give it unless I choose. Inspector Cauldron knows that as well as I."

Billie looked at the inspector, who was evidently unprepared to give this statement the clear denial that she expected to hear. He was less than sure that Webber's cynical attitude, interpreted at its worst, was yet not beyond the reach of the law. He knew that if a baby should fall into a brook eighteen inches deep, and a dozen people should stand round idly watching it drown, a word of sarcastic condemnation from an indignant coroner would be the worst penalty they would incur. He confined himself to the first part of Webber's assertion when he replied: "I should say you've done nothing right, and everything wrong; and. now you're talking about throwing away the one chance you've got. There's no doubt you supplied whatever drug has been used to poison Mr. Boyle, and that you knew what it was, so that you could bring the antidote here. And you look at the state he's getting into—"

Webber interrupted shrewdly: "Doesn't that sound as though I wasn't giving him the right thing...? Why not get a good doctor in?"

Boyle's voice came from the bed, the words slow and slurred indistinctly, showing how rapidly his condition was degenerating: "A doctor wouldn't be any good.... Better give him the promise he wants, Inspector. You'll get nothing without.... What about ten thousand, Webber, instead of five?"

But Webber was in a condition of frightened obstinacy, which could be moved neither by persuasion, nor bribery, nor threat. His mind held to one central fact, among many hesitations and fears: if Boyle should die without having made accusation against Shorter in a form which could be legally used, it would be very difficult for the police to proceed, even against Shorter himself, and much more so against anyone who might be suspected of complicity in the alleged crime.

Beyond that, he felt that Boyle alive was of more danger than Boyle dead, even though no statement were made; and at the back of his mind was the conviction that, if he stood out long enough, the police would come to his own terms. He thought they had too much to lose, though he did not guess how much it had come to be.

Inspector Cauldron felt that there was no further argument he could urge, and he was resolved that he would not give a pledge that he might be powerless to keep.

He looked at the man who now lay with closed eyes as though already in too deep a torpor, after the exertion of the few slow words he had uttered, to be aware of what was passing round him. "Miss Wingrove," he said, "this is beyond me. You'd better phone the superintendent, and ask him to come at once."

CHAPTER XX.

WEBBER DECIDES

SUPERINTENDENT BACKWASH, having seen Sir James, wearing an expression of outraged dignity, led from the room by a stolid sergeant, who would have taken charge of the Archbishop of Canterbury, or his own brother, in the same unemotional manner, delayed only to speak to Chief Inspector Tolbooth, and arrange for him to examine the two other men who were already in custody, which few would be better able to do.

"If you get anything out of the bounders, Tolbooth, you might phone me at once at Rivers Square—Tavistock 6099's the number. It's hard to say what might be useful, but the more they each think the others are talking, the more likely they are to talk themselves. And if I haven't got this case looking rather different from what it does now by when Sir Henry comes back—"

There was no need to finish the sentence.

Tolbooth was a man of few words, apart from those which his official duties required, and those few were not often of a sanguine kind. He said, "It'll look different when it's cooked up"—and the superintendent understood, not merely that he had the chief inspector's sympathy and support, which would be of no decisive value should he come a cropper in what he was trying to do, but that he had the approval of a judgement the shrewdness of which had become proverbial at the Yard. It was a support he needed for the ordeal he had to face.

He took less time even than he had said to reach Rivers Square, where Mrs. Jepson showed him into the bedroom, the occupants of which had become silent as they waited for him to appear.

His first glance was at Boyle, and when he saw him lying silent and apathetic, and the grey lines of the set face, he said: "There's one thing certain. We can't take the responsibility of keeping Mr. Boyle without proper medical attention." He raised his voice to continue: "If you'd like your own doctor called in, Mr. Boyle—" But there was no sign that the words penetrated the stupor in which the sick man lay, and he went on: "Miss Wingrove, you might telephone for one of our police surgeons—Biddle would be the best, if he can be got—to come here at once; and tell them to let him know what the case is like, and that he can have any specialists here that he thinks well. But they've got to jump to it, if they're to do any good."

He turned to Webber as Billie left the room, and said quietly: "I'm not going to waste words with you. The time's come when this gang's going to be broken up, and if some of them end on the gallows I shall be more pleased than surprised. We're taking statements from your friends Guttins and Sinster now. How many more we shall have roped in when we've finished hearing what they've got to say, I dare say you can make as good guess as I, but we expect to be rather full.

"We've got Sir James Shorter locked up, and I suppose you've got sense enough to see that we shouldn't have done that if we didn't mean to go the whole way. We've got plenty on you to put you away for a long stretch, but what we shall do will depend on yourself. That's not a promise. It's just information as to what we intend to do. I make no promise at all. I give you three minutes to think it over, and at the end of that time you'll either be doing all you can to save Mr. Boyle's life, or you'll be on your way to the cells."

Webber said obstinately: "It's no use trying to bluff me like that. I don't care who you've arrested. I've nothing to do with any gang, and I never had. You can't do anything to me. I've done nothing wrong."

The superintendent answered, as quietly as before: "Have it your own way. But keep your lies for the jury. They don't interest me. I've no more to say. The three minutes is beginning now."

He took out his watch.

He watched the minute hand go twice round its tiny dial and a third time until only fifteen seconds were left and then looked up to say: "Time almost up."

Webber spoke irresolutely and his tone apart from the words that came showed that the game had been nearly won. "I don't want any doctors about if I'm to do what you want."

"That's asking too much now."

"I want to be left alone with Mr. Boyle."

"I can't promise that. He might die. Where should we be then? I'll meet you as far as I can. A doctor shall be in the room but he won't interfere as long as he sees you're doing the right thing."

Webber looked dubious. He did not like the wording of this promise. He asked: "He won't want to interfere with my things? You'll promise that there'll be no interference with my bag? That I shall be allowed to take it away?"

It was the superintendent's turn to pause. But there was too much at stake to risk arousing the renewed obstinacy of an obviously yielding man.

"Yes," he said, "if you get Mr. Boyle round I promise you shall leave here with your bag unexamined as far as we are concerned… but I can't promise anything if he dies and looks to me as though it's touch-and-go now. I should say you can't be too quick in whatever you've got to do."

Webber still stood uncertainly. It was evident that the moment of final decision had come. It was still less than sure what that decision would be when Billie returned to the room. She said: "Dr. Biddle's on his way here now. Chief Inspector Tolbooth wants to talk to you, if you can come. He says he's got some things out of Sinster you'll be interested to hear. And he wanted you to know that they've just brought Humphries in."

The words were not addressed to Webber, but they appeared to have a decisive effect on that irresolute man: He picked up the syringe and began to prepare it for use.

CHAPTER XXI.

Is It Too Late?

THE next two hours were among the most anxious that more than one of those who watched round the bed of the poisoned man had spent in lives which had not been free from stresses of various kinds.

Webber had administered the injection which should have been given more than an hour before, and the reaction, which should have been almost immediately apparent, was slow to come.

Dr. Biddle, sharp-eyed, sardonic, watched silently, chin on hand, from the further side of the room. Inspector Cauldron had explained the position to him in the lounge on his arrival, and he had made his own clear, with customary bluntness. "I don't say you're wrong. These South American poisons are the devil, and there are plenty of which we know little of their effects, and still less of how they can be overcome. If it's so important to get the man talking, I should let the blighter carry on in his own way. That's between ourselves. "Off the record," as the Americans say.

"But it's no use asking me to do anything while this Webber quack's on the job. And as to calling specialists to butt in—why, if I should merely propose it, I should be before the Council for infamous conduct, more likely than not.

"I'll just sit round and watch what happens, and any time you kick Webber out of the room, I'll take over, and do the best I can.... But I don't say I shall be able to do any good. The longer I stay on a back seat, the better pleased I shall be."

Webber, having given the injection, declined to do anything further, not, apparently, from any unwillingness, but because there was nothing further that could be usefully done.

There was little speech among those who watched, and the silence was seldom broken, except by the quarterly striking of the clock of St. Mildred's Church, which stands on the further side of the square. It had a slow and heavy sound in the silent room, emphasizing the fatal passage of the time which seemed so long, and yet to be slipping away so ominously for the drugged man who was the unconscious centre of all their eyes.

It was as the last stroke of midnight died that Dr. Biddle, who was not oblivious of the expression of increasing anxiety on the superintendent's face, said, without appearing to address anyone in particular: "If I were asked, I should be obliged to decline to express my opinion. But, not being asked, and merely thinking aloud, I can't help wondering whether it wouldn't be worth while trying another shot."

Webber turned harassed eyes in his direction. "I daren't do it," he said. "The length of interval is essential, or it has other effects, which might be fatal at once." He added hurriedly: "That's what's said about it. I've no experience. I've never done anything with it before."

"It's best to go by the rules, when you're not sure," Dr. Biddle assented, having been more nearly drawn into direct conversation than he had intended, and then dropped his eyes to the ground, as though it were the carpet to which he spoke.

Webber muttered: "There's another twenty minutes to go yet." He felt Boyle's pulse, as he had done several times before. He added, in a rather more hopeful tone: "I reckon he'll last till then. It's after that we shall know."

Billie rose, saying: "There'll be time to get you all a cup of tea before that." She went out, without waiting for a reply. If they didn't need it, she did! And if Mrs. Jepson were not about, she reckoned she would find what was necessary.

Silence settled again on the room she left. Superintendent Backwash had had time to review the position as it would be if there should be no further word from a dying man, and it was not one to give him a quiet mind, even with the support of the information he had had from Chief Inspector Tolbooth before Dr. Biddle's arrival.

That information was that Guttins had declined to open his mouth to any useful purpose; but Sinster had been easily frightened into voluble speech. He admitted that his car had been used for the distribution of illicit drugs. He gave the address where it was kept, and where quantities of such merchandise would certainly be found, if they had not been removed in the last three hours. He gave the names of several who were concerned in the traffic. He gave other addresses which they frequented. He probably told much less than he knew, omitting such matters as would most gravely involve himself, but what he told would be enough to enable a swift and deadly blow to be struck at the underlings of the gang, and perhaps some who were above them. To secure this, instant action had been taken, even before Tolbooth had phoned to report the measure of his success.

But on the point of greater importance—the complicity of Sir James Shorter—Sinster professed to know nothing. Nor of Boyle. He said the names were strange to him, and Tolbooth was disposed to think that this was a genuine ignorance. It emphasized to Superintendent Backwash's mind, the measure of the safe and easy triumph which might have been his had he taken the surer road.... Now, unless Boyle should speak, and in the right way—well, the more thoroughly he analysed the position, the more hopeless it seemed to be.

If Boyle should die, who would there be whose evidence might avail? Guttins? He might know much or little, but it was clear that he would not talk without more occasion than there would then be. Webber? His attitude, in the same event, would almost certainly be the same.

And they were both under suspicion of criminality. Was it on the word of such men that any jury would convict Sir James Shorter? It was an absurdity to consider. Such a trial would never be allowed. Probably before twenty-four hours were over he would be hearing Sir Henry telling him that an abject apology must he the preliminary to his conduct being submitted to the Home Secretary for such disciplinary action as the occasion required. Well, he could always resign!—as it was more than likely that he was destined to do.

CHAPTER XXII.

THE STATEMENT OF PETER BOYLE

BILLIE had found Mrs. Jepson up, a disturbed woman, disinclined to talk, but showing no unwillingness to prepare a pot of tea and a plate of attractive sandwiches, or to accept Billie's assistance at this domestic enterprise.

"I suppose," she said, as the tray was ready to be taken in, it being the first time she had spoken a needless word, "there's no hope the master'll be having any?"

There was a real anxiety in her voice which Billie had not expected to hear. "I'm afraid not," she answered, "but there seems to be a chance that he may live." And then added, with a confidence she would not have thought of giving a moment before: "I don't know which would be best for him."

Mrs. Jepson said: "He used to be different once." How much did she know or guess?

She picked up the tray, and they went back to the room together.

It was fourteen minutes past the hour. In six minutes the final test would be made. Webber, his eyes on the clock, got up and felt Boyle's pulse again. "It's no worse," he said, with no cheerfulness in the tone. It seemed to those who looked on that the lifted hand dropped back even more heavily than before.

Billie said: "I expect he'll come round all right. He's got through the dangerous time, hasn't he?"

No one answered this hopefully ignorant forecast, but they accepted the tea and sandwiches with suitable gratitude, and had substantially reduced the liberal quantity which had been provided before Webber stepped up to the bed, bared the arm of the unconscious man, and drove in the needle.

Those who watched during the next ten minutes could see that the drug did not act with its previous celerity. Yet act it did. A more natural colour came slowly to the rigid face. Then a hand moved.

Webber felt the weak pulse again, and said in a relieved voice: "Yes, it's acting now."

It seemed that Webber, having once been persuaded to that course of action, had been anxious that he should not fail. It gave Superintendent Backwash a new source of satisfaction, for it had not been the least of his fears during the last two hours that Webber might be double-crossing him in a way which might be beyond proof—gaining thereby the credit of having done his best to save the life of the poisoned man, while avoiding the risk to himself which might follow from any statement that he might make.

But it became evident now that consciousness, and some power of movement, were returning, however slowly. After a few further minutes the eyes opened. They gained intelligence. The head lifted slightly. It seemed that Boyle was regaining knowledge of who were round him—probably memory of what had happened.

Billie asked: "Do you think he could take anything?"

"He mustn't try to eat. Not till tomorrow," Webber answered. "It would be fatal, more likely than not."

"I was thinking of some tea."

"We might try that," Webber replied doubtfully. "It couldn't do any harm."

Wondering whether she had proposed something which would destroy his returning hope, Superintendent Backwash watched her approach the sick man and hold a cup of tea to his stiffened lips. He drank with difficulty, but, having swallowed some, he became eager for, more. Animation increased.

A quarter of an hour later the superintendent said: "I don't want to hurry you, Mr. Boyle, but I'm ready any time you feel fit to talk."

"I understand," came the slow, slurred words of the reply. "You shall have what you want. But you mustn't rush me. I want to think."

A minute later he asked: "Where's Shorter now? You won't—you know what I mean. He's got powerful friends."

"Sir James Shorter is now at Scotland Yard. You can be sure we shan't let him go, if you give us the information we need."

"You mean you've arrested him?" The voice was sceptical.

"He's not arrested yet. He's detained."

The careful distinction seemed to give Boyle assurance of the truth of what he had been told. He looked relieved as he turned to Webber to ask: "I shall live now?"

"You'll be all right after you've had another injection."

"You can depend absolutely," the superintendent assured him, "upon Webber giving you that at the right time. He'll give us—and you—all the help he can."

"Yes," Boyle answered—"yes, I understand that." He looked at Webber again to ask: "How much of it have you got? You're not short?"

"I've got the full quantity—plenty for the last dose."

"That's all I wanted to know. I'll tell you what you want now."

"I think Miss Wingrove does shorthand," Inspector Cauldron observed.

"There'll be plenty of paper in the next room."

"I can take down," Billie admitted, "but I'm out of practice now. There's a typewriter in the next room. Why shouldn't I take it direct?"

"That," the superintendent agreed, "will be far the best way." He saw that they would save the time that transcription requires, while getting the actual words of whatever statement would be made—and after it had been made it could not be read over and signed too quickly, in view of the condition of the man with whom they were dealing.

Inspector Cauldron and Billie left the room together and returned with the typewriter and paper which the occasion required.

Boyle, now appearing to be in almost normal control of his faculties, asked anxiously: "If I give you the whole tale, you'll hold on to Shorter? You won't be content with the others, and let him go?"

"No," Superintendent Backwash answered. "You just give us the dope. We won't let him go." There was a grimness in the tone in which these words were spoken which seemed to satisfy Boyle's anxious doubt. "Very well," he said, "let's begin."

After that he dictated, speaking somewhat slowly at first, but soon at a pace which taxed the speed of Billie's accustomed fingers. The listening policemen did not interrupt. They were being too richly fed. It was three-quarters of an hour later that the narrative ceased with the words: "Well, you've got it now. Read it over to me, and I'll sign it once."

Billie read it over. It was an astonishing document. It gave the personnel, high and low, of the Mildew Gang—the addresses from which they worked, their sources of supply, their methods of distribution, the names of their foreign agents and correspondents, even particulars of how their funds could be traced, and of more than one murder which had been committed for their own safety or to punish breaches of discipline or honesty among themselves. In particular, it was alleged that Sir James Shorter had previously poisoned a Member of Parliament who had been widely known as a philanthropic public worker, because he had accidentally come upon evidence of Sir James's association with the gang. In that case the same drug had been used as that from which Boyle was now suffering. The unfortunate man had been found dead in bed, and "heart failure" had been the verdict on his unexpected end.

Throughout the whole statement Boyle made no effort to except or excuse himself. He gave facts concisely, and they were damning for all concerned. By the time it had been read over, and he had signed it and initialled each separate sheet, he was showing signs of extreme physical exhaustion, as well as some recurrence of the previous symptoms—the difficulty in speaking clearly or moving freely—which the antidote had temporarily relieved.

"He'll be all right," Webber said, "after the next shot. But it's too soon to be giving it yet."

"You'll pull him through, and we'll do all I said, and perhaps a bit more," Superintendent Backwash answered coldly. He loathed the man, but the service he has rendering could not be denied, and faith must be kept, even with such as he.

CHAPTER XXIII.

The Decisive Action of Peter Boyle

As the last sheet of the precious document was blotted, Superintendent Backwash folded them and slipped them into his breast-pocket. "There'll be no rest tonight for me," he said cheerfully, "and not much for you, I'm afraid, Cauldron. But I'd like a few words with you in the next room.... Miss Wingrove, you'd better stay here till Inspector Cauldron comes back, and after that the sooner you get home and get some rest, the better I should say it will be." He went out without waiting for a reply, Inspector Cauldron following him, and continued as soon as they were alone: "I don't trust Webber an inch, but we've got to keep faith with him. My promise was that he should be free to go, without having his bag examined, as soon as we know said Boyle's life. Well, I suppose that'll be plain, one way or other, when he's given the next injection, or not long after. That's where Biddle comes in. It's up to him to say when he thinks Boyle's definitely out of danger.

"I say we've got to play fair. But we mustn't do more than that. While Webber's here, he mustn't communicate with *anyone*. Not on any pretext whatever. When he does go, I'll arrange for him to be looked after closely enough for him not to do any great harm. And it mayn't matter as much by then. I hope to have quite a few of the gang out of their beds before morning. They're going to be some surprised men.... But he's your charge till then. And, of course, so is Boyle. He didn't seem to care how much he was giving himself away, so long as he was putting salt on Shorter's tail.... Ask Miss Wingrove to ring up Tolbooth to say I'm on the way with goods, and that he's to get everyone together he can at this hour for a busy night.... It looks like being the best day's work that I've ever done, and that goes for you too."

"I can't say I've done much. It's Miss Wingrove really who pulled it off."

"Have it your own way. But we put some finishing touches, which she wouldn't have been able to do."

With these words he went, and two minutes later Billie was phoning Chief Inspector Tolbooth, who heard the good news without expressing any particular emotion concerning it. His mind appeared to be set upon speaking to the superintendent himself, and when he learned that that was impossible, he answered: "Oh, well, he'll find out when he gets here. That'll be soon enough."

"There's something happened," she thought, "which he wouldn't tell me. Something important, I think. I hope it was something good. It almost sounded as though it was a joke that he mustn't tell."

She communicated this impression to Inspector Cauldron, whom she met in the passage between the two rooms, as though he had been coming to speak to her, but he attached no importance to it.

"It's just Tolbooth's way," he replied, in the tone of one whose thoughts were on more important things—"and, anyway, what can it matter? With that statement in his pocket, Backwash has got everything where he wants it to be."

"I suppose he'll get all sorts of praise and—whatever superintendents do get for this? And you've really done a lot more than he."

"I hadn't noticed that. I'd been watching you. And, anyway, that's not fair. He risked his whole career when he gave Shorter bed and breakfast tonight.... But I came out to make sure that you weren't slipping off home."

"Really? Don't you think I've done about enough for one day? Even for the C.I.D.?"

"You've done more than enough, but I don't want it to be the last day's work that you'll ever do.... Webber gave me the hint that it isn't safe. He says they may have Guttins, but there's no knowing what orders he gave before he was taken up.... He says your rooms will be watched for sure; and they know you're here now, more likely than not."

"I should say they'll have more important matters to think of now."

"So they may before this time tomorrow. Or, at least, I don't exactly mean that. There couldn't be anything. But don't you see that we want to run them in before they've got any suspicion that we're on their track? And meanwhile they'll go on as though nothing's happened. And I don't want them to spend their last hours making any trouble for you."

"It's very good of you to worry about me," Billie answered, in a better tone than the words would naturally bear, "but I don't see why you should. And I don't believe Webber does. Not a straw. I shouldn't take any notice of him. Not to stay out of bed when I'm as tired as I am now."

"Well, just hear what he's got to say. He's a mean rat, but he wants to, soap up to us now, and I think he knows what he's talking about."

"There wasn't much about him in Mr. Boyle's statement."

"No, lucky for him. He may have left him out on purpose, but I should guess it was only that there was so much else to get in."

"Well, I'll hear what he's got to say."

They went back to the bedroom together, but it was not Webber, but Boyle, who brought up the subject at once.

"Mrs. Risdon," he began, with a sarcastic inflexion on the false name by which she had introduced herself to him, "I don't owe you anything. You've done more mischief than all the officers of the C.I.D. have been able to manage in the last five years. And if we go far enough back, I reckon it's through you that I'm lying here. But as things are now, there's no need that they should lose the best spy that they ever had.... If you try going back now to wherever you really live, I reckon you'll be dead before morning, more likely than not.... But if Inspector Cauldron will be kind enough to let Mr. Webber telephone from the next room, without being overheard, he'll send orders from me that'll make it all right for you. That is, if you're sure Shorter's under lock and key. I couldn't promise anything apart from that. There might be some taking orders from him."

"There's no doubt about that," Inspector Cauldron answered.

"He'll be locked up safe enough till the superintendent gets back, and he's hardly likely to let him out with what he's got in his pocket now. But I can't let Webber phone. He must tell me who to ring up, and what to say."

"I was to be free to leave—" Webber began angrily, and was interrupted with: "So you will be when the time comes, and that's when you've finished putting Mr. Boyle on his feet. You can bank on that. But you'll do no phoning till then. Not even to help us. Tell me who to ring up, and I'll manage that."

"It wouldn't be any good. They'd know it wasn't the right voice."

Inspector Cauldron received this explanation with some inward scepticism. He judged that there were still those whose exposure Boyle had spared, from whatever motive. Or the difficulty might be no more than that Webber did not wish it to be seen how far he was known to the gang. Anyway, he was equally resolved that there should neither be risk for Billie nor evasion of the orders he had received that Webber should not have any outside communication.

Boyle cut the knot, before he had resolved what he would do, by saying: "It's not worth arguing. I'll have a word myself that you can all hear. What does it matter now?"

Webber put the bedside telephone into his hands, and while Inspector Cauldron hesitated as to whether even this measure of communication with the underlings of the gang did not against the spirit of the instructions he had received, and decided that it must be risked, or rather that no risk was involved, Boyle gave a number which Inspector Cauldron was careful not to forget, though it was to prove a needless precaution, all it could disclose being in Boyle's statement already, and said: "Repton speaking. Dexter or Rhodes must report at once to Tavistock 6099." Having said this, he lay back and closed his eyes, as though exhausted by the effort he had made, but he roused himself when the telephone bell rang a few minutes later, and had his hand on the instrument before Inspector Cauldron could cross the room to take it. "I think this is for me," he said.... "Yes. Repton speaking. The last order for removal is cancelled.... Yes, absolutely.... Yes, but that won't arise.... Yes, you have done well.... Not for an hour.... There would be no excuse after that.... There has been a friendly settlement of the whole matter.... Then tell him not to think. It's a dangerous habit."

His voice during the conversation had regained a hard and minatory quality which must have been customary when giving orders to the lawless elements that he had ruled and paid, rewarded or punished, in accordance with their services to the gang. For the minutes during which he spoke he may have forgotten that it was a position that he would never occupy again.

"Inspector," he said, "within half an hour Miss Wingrove will be as safe as ever she was in her life, so, if she did something for me when she got Webber here, we can call it quits about that. Not that I'd say she hadn't done enough in other ways to deserve anything she was going to get.... But I'm sure that Shorter's a hanging job you'll have no trouble from me.... I say half an hour, but I gave them an hour, to be on the right side, and she'd better stay here till four o'clock, and then take a taxi home."

"Very well," Inspector Cauldron agreed; "I'm sure Miss Wingrove won't object to that. It's always best to be on the safe side."

"I think," Billie said, "it's a lot of fuss about nothing. But it would be silly not to agree." She settled down in the armchair she had occupied before, with a resolution not to go to sleep, as it would have been so easy to do.

Dr. Biddle rose. "As I suppose I am not a subject of the peculiar kind of interest of which we have been hearing, and Mr. Boyle seems to be doing very well without calling me in, there doesn't seem to be any good reason why I shouldn't go home to bed."

Webber said: "He'll be all right now, after the next dose."

"I expect," Inspector Cauldron observed, "you have had a hard day."

"I most often do," the police surgeon said, in his sharper manner. It was clear that no one else thought it necessary that he should stay. Neither did he. With little ceremony of leave-taking, he went out, and the room settled into silence.

So it came that Billie was still there when the time arrived for the final injection to be given, and she watched, with no great interest, while Webber filled the syringe and approached the bedside.

It had become evident that Boyle's condition was again critical. He lay as though unconscious, and the grey pallor of his face which had been indicative of his earlier relapse was again apparent. But Webber was not perturbed; he knew that the poison did not work with a gradually diminishing virulence. It persisted for a time, and then ceased. On the other hand, the antidote was of a periodically diminishing potency. After the mental excitement and exertion of the last hours, it was natural that Boyle should be in a condition of extremity. Yet, even so, Webber had confident knowledge that the next injection would sustain his life until the poison should have lost its power.

As he approached the bed the lids of the sick man's eyes opened, slowly and stiffly. His voice was hardly audible as he asked: "Is that all you've got?"

"Yes; but there's plenty here. It's the last dose you'll need."

Boyle's further hand was raised slightly, and fell back. It appeared to be too stiff or feeble for a greater exertion. The motion was repeated, somewhat more strongly. Then, as with one final supreme exertion, it came over, dashing the syringe away, even as the needle had touched the flesh. It fell, broken, upon the floor. Boyle's voice was almost at its normal strength as he said: "Did you think I should live after all I've told? But Shorter'll get—" The voice sank suddenly, but the sentence was clear, even though its conclusion could not be heard.

Inspector Cauldron had stepped forward quickly to recover the broken syringe; but it was evident that neither it nor its spilled contents would be of any further availability.

"Was that really," he asked, "all you'd got?"

"Yes. I brought the full quantity required. That's how it's done up, so that no mistake shall be made," Webber answered, showing a small cardboard box with compartments in which the capsules had been held.

"But you've got more you can fetch?"

Webber plainly hesitated. Did he still think that if Boyle were dead it would be better for him?

"Yes," he admitted at last. "But it won't do any good. It will be too late. Nothing'd save him now."

"We've got to try. I'll come with—no, I must stay here. Billie," he went on, apparently unconscious of the familiarity of the Christian name which he had been invited vainly to use on a previous occasion, "you'd better go with Mr. Webber, and make sure that no time's lost. You'll be able to explain, if any of our men should try interfering with him. There'll be a lot of rounding up done tonight.... And he'll be able to vouch for you with his own riff-raff, if there should be any trouble with them."

Billie heard this proposal with a distaste which she did not show. She was exhausted by the excitements of a long day, and her strongest inclination was to go back to her own room. She had reluctantly stayed for the last hour at the call of a prudence she could not deny. But to set out again— Yet she saw that what she was now asked to do was not without adequate reason, nor was it requiring a greater sacrifice of her own comfort than was being made that night by many other members of much rounding up before another morning would dawn. And it would be done by men who had been on duty during the day, and might have been summoned to return just as they were turning in for a hard-earned sleep.

She saw that it was a matter of imperative urgency that Webber should fetch the drug, and that Inspector Cauldron could not properly leave the confessed criminal and would-be suicide, whose evidence might be of supreme importance in the prosecution of those whom his statement implicated. She saw also that Webber might easily be caught in the wide-flung net which the C.I.D. would cast abroad for such as he during the night, or, more probably, he might, with or without such excuse, be deliberately slow to return, being well content if he should be too late. Her presence would avert these possibilities; while, if there should be any remaining peril to herself from any members of the gang whom Boyle's last orders might not have reached, she would be safer in the company of one of themselves, who could explain the position which had developed, than if she were to start off alone to her own room—an address which she knew they already had.

"Yes; I'll go," she said, trying to keep the weariness out of her voice.

Webber began: "There's no need"—and then cleared the scowl from his face to conclude: "It doesn't matter one way or other to me."

"And you can't be too quick about it," Cauldron added sharply.

Webber made no reply, but took up his hat, and Billie and he went out together without further words.

But she was only in the descending lift when she became aware of a strong disinclination to go out into the night with her unattractive companion. Whether it arose from her dislike and distrust of the man, or the physical weariness which she was endeavouring to overcome, the fact was that she was more conscious of fear than she had been on more than one previous occasion when peril had been more apparent than it was then.

She had to remind herself that she had set out a few hours before knowing that she was the object of the vengeance of the ruthless gang against which she worked. Then she had put the thought boldly aside, remembering only the deadly urgency of the errand on which she went. Now the urgency was no less, though it was no longer at the desire of the poisoned man, and her own danger might be regarded as a past tale.... "I suppose," she said, as the lift stopped at the ground floor, "that we go to Bright's Passage?"

"Yes," he said shortly. He had no intention of disclosing an address at which he had stores of drugs, of which, even now, it might be possible for him to retain control. It was an address which Boyle had not given, of which even he might not know; and it was true that another set of the capsules was in the office safe, and that it would take no longer—or, at least, not much—to get them from there.

"We mayn't get a taxi quickly at this time of night," he said, as they emerged into a silent street, in which a light rain was falling.

"I expect we shall. There's a stand round the corner I noticed it as I came," she answered, with resolute cheer fullness. She was not dressed for rain or the chill of the night wind. She thought angrily: "I mayn't get murdered—I don't suppose there ever was much real danger of that—but I'm going to get an infernal cold, more likely than not." At the moment, it almost seemed the worse choice of the two—a feeling which was not relieved when they turned the corner and found that no taxis were on the stand.

But next moment a car came slowly along their side of the street. There was no need to hail it. It pulled up beside them. A voice called: "That you; Mr. Webber?"

Webber evidently knew the speaker. He answered:

"Yes, Clements. I want to Get to Fenchurch Street—Bright's Passage—to my office. It's a most urgent matter. Can you drive this young lady and me?"

An arm reached back, opening the rear door. "I dare say I can. But better get in to talk. There's no sense in standing in that rain."

Webber stood back to make way for Billie, who got in, though with some doubt of the wisdom of what she did. She was puzzled rather than alarmed. How should anyone who knew Webber be waiting there? That he was another member of the gang was a simple guess. But what brought him there? The telephone conversation which Guttins had had after entering the flat came to her mind, and was the true explanation of the mere knowledge of Webber's presence; but the fact that the car had been sent was owing to other events of the night, which it was impossible for her to guess.

CHAPTER XXIV.

TROUBLE AT SCOTLAND YARD

WHEN Superintendent Backwash got back to his own office, he was not surprised to find Chief Inspector Tolbooth waiting for him, but he was aware of the unexpected when, in place of the bustling activities which he had expected him to originate, he saw that he was occupied in no more active manner than whistling softly to himself, while tapping a pencil, now head, now point, on the desk before him.

But he knew Tolbooth to be a man who would appear unhurried in any crisis, and his own thoughts were preoccupied by the importance of the document that his pocket held.

When Tolbooth looked up, with an expression on his face that was difficult to read, and asked laconically, "Good luck?" he answered: "Rather. I dare say some people would think more than I had any right to expect. I've got—"

"Well, you'll need it. Sir Henry's back."

"How on earth—"

"Oh, Forsyth saw to that. Got him on the phone before he came to see Shorter here, at a good guess."

"Then he knows everything by now?"

"I wouldn't say that. Probably thinks he does. He's been quite active for him. Got a conference on now—Wilts, Rattray, Braddon, and Tamm. I'm not in favour just now.... But he'd better tell you what he's been doing. He wants you to go in at once."

"Well, he can't have done much harm by now. Held up everything, I suppose. But he'll sit up when he reads

As he spoke, he drew out the bundle of foolscap sheets which had been bulging his breast pocket. They had a formidable appearance. Boyle used paper of good quality.

Tolbooth said: "Yes?" reflectively. He added inconsequently: "Sir Henry isn't a bad sort." And then: "Neither are you." His pencil resumed its tapping.

Superintendent Backwash went on to the Assistant Commissioner's room. He was confident in the success of what he had done, but impatient at the delay which explanations would mean, at a moment when instant action was so imperatively required. He told himself, in the brief moment before he opened the door of a room in which he could hear sounds of a loud discussion, that he must have patience. Loss of temper might mean greater loss of time rather than less.

As he entered, he heard Superintendent Rattray, say, "...Adam Street raid went to his head, if you ask me," and knew that his conduct had been under discussion in no friendly atmosphere. But Rattray was like that to everyone. It would be foolish to allow himself to be annoyed by words which had not been meant for his ears.

"Sit down, Backwash," the Assistant Commissioner began, rather as though he were addressing a convicted criminal than one of the most important and reliable of his famous staff. "I'm afraid you've made a very serious blunder. Very serious indeed. How an officer of your experience could act in such a manner, and without consultation—"

"You were away, sir, or of course I should have placed the matter before you. But it didn't seem to me to admit of delay. Actually, Tolbooth knew and agreed. But of course the responsibility was entirely mine."

"So it appears. I have already admonished Tolbooth, but I am rather surprised that you should bring his name—"

"I think he deserves some share of any credit—"

"*Credit?* Don't you understand that, if you be allowed to resign, you may call yourself a very fortunate man? That will be for the Home Secretary to decide. But I must require you, in the first instance, to attend upon Sir James Shorter, and make him a most abject apology, emphasizing the fact that you acted entirely upon your own authority, and that you have placed yourself in the hands of your superiors for such disciplinary action as may be considered appropriate."

"I couldn't possibly do that."

"Then you must consider yourself suspended—"

"If you'd just look at this document—"

"What does it purport to be?"

"Boyle's confession. It's the end of the Mildew Gang."

"You mean Boyle has admitted his own criminality?"

"Yes. It is a very detailed statement."

"How do you bring Sir James Shorter into this?"

"They lunched together today—yesterday—and Shorter tried poisoning him. It's scarcely a couple of hours since we could feel sure that he'd pull through."

"What evidence of that have you, apart from Boyle's statement?"

"None directly, at present. Or, rather, there's the fact that Webber—but that's a long story. We shall have plenty by this time tomorrow, if we call make a few arrests before they have time to get together, and agree what they're going to say."

"You mean to tell me that, with all your experience, you accept the statement of a confessed criminal that a man of Sir James Shorter's position and reputation is implicated with him, without confirmation, when it's a hundred to one that he's bringing in the name of an innocent man to cover his own misdeeds?"

"I don't think it's as simple as that. And the fact that Shorter's got a good reputation doesn't seem to me to be at all conclusive. We've known for a long while that the gang was being run by people it would be hard to suspect. There was Mildew himself. And Boyle—though I don't say his reputation was anything like Shorter's—wasn't an easy guess."

"The mistake you've been making, Backwash, is that you've jumped from the idea that it's probable that heads of the Mildew Gang are people of outward respectability to thinking that it's probable that people of outward respectability are heads of the Mildew Gang. And so you've let Boyle give you such a twist that we may find it's impossible to prosecute even him, because of it all coming out, and the fools it would make us look shouldn't wonder if that's just what he's been aiming to do."

"I dare say it looks rather like that, but you're assuming that Shorter's innocent, and I'm sure he's not.... I'll ask you to do this, sir, before you come to any conclusion. Have Shorter up here, and let me ask him a few questions before he knows what we've got in this document, and if he doesn't get caught in some statements that we can prove to be false in the next twenty-four hours—"

The telephone bell interrupted this proposal. The Assistant Commissioner took up the instrument. "Cauldron?" he said. "No. Tell him I can't be interrupted now. I don't care how urgent it is. Let Tolbooth take it. He's talked to Tolbooth already? Then what does he mean by interrupting—"

But Sir Henry was interrupted in another way as he asked this, for, with no ceremony, Chief Inspector Tolbooth came into the room.

"There are two things," he said, "that Cauldron has just reported which I think you should know at once. One is that Boyle's dead. Committed suicide, in a way. It seems that he didn't care what became of himself so long as he had his revenge on Shorter, and I suppose he reckoned that, if he died, Shorter would be sure to hang. But that will keep.

"The other matter's more urgent. It appears that some members of the gang had instructions to assassinate Miss Wingrove, on account of what she's been finding out about them lately. Boyle cancelled these instructions, and said she'd be safe now, so long as Shorter couldn't alter his orders. Now she's gone off with Webber, one of the gang, nobody knows where. Cauldron was wild with anxiety when he heard how matters stand here."

"Cauldron," Superintendent Backwash interposed, "is always worrying about Miss Wingrove. It's a point on which he's a bit weak in the head. But if Boyle said she would be safe now—"

"He only said as long as we'd got Shorter here."

The two officers stared at one another in mutual misunderstanding. Then Tolbooth said: "I didn't think you'd have been talking all this time without being told that. Sir James Shorter was released from here two or three hours ago."

The room had become silent during these exchanges. More than one of the experienced officers present had already become doubtful of where truth and consequent wisdom lay. They watched noncommittally. Sir Henry's face now showed a mingling of uneasiness and bewilderment which did nothing to encourage those who had been disposed to support the course he had taken.

Then the silence was broken by three distinct words from Superintendent Backwash, such as had surely never been addressed to any Assistant Commissioner in that room before: *"You infernal fool!"*

Sir Henry Bracken does not shine in this narrative. The ideal of doing nothing rather than risk an error, which is the bane both of the Civil Service and party-political life, had misled him into the very position which, it was his first care to avoid. But he had the manners and instincts of the class to which he belonged. He heard that amazing insult alike to himself and the dignified office he held without loss of temper or self-control.

"Superintendent Backwash," he said formally, "after that re-mark, you will understand that the course of resignation is no longer open. Your conduct will be dealt with in another way."

Superintendent Backwash was aware that he had been guilty of a breach of discipline which was beyond excuse. He had placed himself in the wrong, which he had felt some confidence that others would be unable to do.

Sobered by this consciousness, he replied in an altered voice: "I'm sincerely sorry, sir. It was an expression I should not have used. I withdraw and apologize. But I've no intention of resigning. If you'll please understand that I don't wish to say it rudely, I think your own resignation is a far greater probability. It isn't only that Shorter will have to be arrested again. It's the probability that he'll have used these hours of freedom to warn his gang, and half the evi-dences on which I relied will be hidden or destroyed It's going to make the coup far less simple and complete than I hoped it would be.

"But it isn't only that. I take back what I said about Cauldron fussing over Miss Wingrove. When he heard that Shorter was loose, I don't wonder he felt alarmed. If you'll listen to me now, sir, in spite of everything that's occurred—"

For a moment this. appeal was met with the silence of indeci-sion. Then Sir Henry looked over to where, at the further end of the table, Superintendent Tamm had been turning over the pages of Boyle's statement and assimilating their significance with the facil-ity which long experience gives.

He passed it up, saying, as he did so: "If I were you, sir, I'd have a look at page four, paragraph three, first. And if we send a squad to MacWhirter's warehouse—well, they may be in time, or they may not. I should call it an even chance."

CHAPTER XXV.

ORDERS MUST BE OBEYED

THE car into which Billie had been invited was a small four-seater saloon. She and Webber occupied the rear seats. The man he had addressed as Clements was alone in front. It was not an ideal position for conversation, but enabled it to be carried on without much difficulty, if both parties were so inclined; and it appeared that Webber wished, and Clements showed no disinclination, to talk.

Billie, glad to be out of the rain, but warily distrustful of her companions, as her previous car experiences gave her good reason to be, was alert both of eyes and ears for any indications of what might be expected from them; but there was at first little, or nothing, to support her instinctive fear.

The coming dawn did not give sufficient light for her to judge what manner of man Clements might be. She could see that he was not a liveried, and she did not think him to be a professional, driver. His formal "Mister" to Webber, which was not reciprocated, suggested some admitted inferiority of social caste or business position. That, on a balance of probabilities, was how she would prefer it to be.

Webber asked: "How did you guess I should be there, needing a lift?"

"Reynolds heard where you were from Guttins. Reynolds sent me to wait for you. Mr. MacWhirter wants to see you at once."

"Well—I don't know about that. As soon as I'm free—"

"I don't know much about it. And I don't want to butt in. But it's something urgent. There were special orders issued an hour ago."

"Yes. About one matter. I heard that. But it doesn't concern me."

"I dare say not," Clements replied indifferently. Actually, they were talking about different things. Webber had in mind the order which Boyle had issued for Billie's safety, which, on the knowledge he had, appeared to be the only one of high authority which could have been given. He could not guess that Shorter, returned to the seclusion of his own fireside, had summoned his butler, to whom, in that secure privacy, he had said a few pregnant words, on hearing which the man had gone off to his own pantry, and had a telephone conversation with another butler, of an apparently innocent character, which had started many activities before morning came. They were not matters with which Shorter could be connected in any way. He had been quietly at home, after the monstrous experience he had endured, and been in communication with none. What connection could there be between such a man and the movements of criminals and drug-traffickers during the night?

Webber persisted: "I don't know why Mr. MacWhirter should want to see me at this hour of the night."

"Well, he does. I don't know beyond that."

Webber was silent for the next two minutes, and then said: "This isn't the best way to Fenchurch Street, is it?" and Billie thought there was alarm in his voice.

"No," the man answered readily, and in the same friendly, indifferent tone as before. "I can't take you there till I get Reynolds' leave. We're going to MacWhirter's first. But it won't make so much difference. Not half an hour, anyway."

The name brought an unpleasant recollection to Billie. The statement she had typed had mentioned a warehouse of that name on the riverside, where, Boyle had alleged, those who fell into Shorter's disfavour, or whom he thought too dangerous to be allowed to live, were quietly drugged, and their stripped bodies committed to the muddy tides of the Thames.

It was not an address to which any girl who knew she had been sentenced to death by the gang would wish to be taken, but Billie must find such confidence as she could from remembering that Boyle had cancelled the sentence, and that Webber did not appear to be conducting her there. Whether from a genuine desire to hurry back to Rivers Square with the remedy so desperately needed, or more selfish motives, he seemed unwilling to go himself.

She found surer ground for comfort in recollecting that Shorter was lodged securely at Scotland Yard, and that Superintendent Backwash should be there before now, and likely to be acting without an instant's delay on the information the statement gave. Probably the police would be there before they could arrive! It would not be a matter of Webber vouching for her, but of her speaking for him, so that he should not be hindered in the errand which he had undertaken! She saw the wisdom of the precaution which Cauldron had used in sending them out together....

"I can't agree to that," Webber was saying. "It's a matter of life and death that I lose no time."

Clements appeared to hesitate. "You make it very awkward for me," he said. "You know what orders are."

"But, when he understands the position, you'll find it's what Reynolds would wish me to do."

"So *you* say. But it's I who should be in the soup if it turned out wrong."

"Then you must put us down, and I'll get a taxi from here."

"You know I couldn't do that. You say you've got something urgent, but I can tell you that there's something else urgent going on that you mayn't know."

"I think I know all that's happened, probably more than Reynolds himself. I'm quite willing to see them as soon as I'm free from what ought to come first."

"Well, we'll be there in a few minutes now."

"I must still insist that you stop the car. Reynolds has no right to give orders to me. I suppose you know that."

"Of course he hasn't. He wouldn't say that he has. He's acting from orders higher up, as we all do."

"I heard the only order that can have been issued tonight, which Reynolds would be obliged to obey. It was about Miss Wingrove's safety, and nothing else."

"You're wrong there. That order got a sock in the jaw about ten minutes after it came through. There's some lively things happening, if you ask me. But I take orders; I don't take sides."

There was one thing in this cryptic statement of which Billie did not like the sound, and others of which she was less than sure. She had felt for some minutes that she might do well to join the conversation, and now she struck in boldly: "If you prefer outsides to insides, Mr. Clements, you might do well to keep away from MacWhirter's warehouse tonight."

There was astonishment in the voice that answered her: "Now what might you mean by that?"

"I mean the insides of jails."

"I don't know who the hell you are, or what concern of yours it can be, but I'll tell you I'm no more concerned about jails than you. I never do anything wrong, and I'm doing nothing wrong now."

"Then a gentleman of your record should be particularly careful to keep away from MacWhirter's warehouse just now."

"When I know who you are, I'll understand better how to take that."

Webber, in a voice of nervous agitation, spoke in the same breath: "Miss Wingrove, you'd better leave this to me."

Clements heard his question answered as it was asked. The name was evidently familiar to him. He stared at Billie in a way she disliked, as though she were a curiosity in herself, or in where she was. "Oh," he said. "I understand now."

He turned to give his undivided attention to the driving wheel, as though there were nothing more to be said. His pace, rapid before, increased, and the gentleman who never did anything wrong overran the traffic lights more than once in the empty streets of the dawn.

Webber repeated nervously: "Please, Miss Wingrove, leave this to me."

His agitation was evident, and though she could not understand fully what was in his mind, she realized that he might have knowledge she did not share, and that her interposition had not, so far, been favourable in its effect.

Webber's dilemma was acute. He saw that she had been on the edge of speaking words which might have been fatal to him, if not to her.

He did not know the full extent of the peril to which they drove, being ignorant of Shorter's release. He had the same half-expectation as she that the police might be at MacWhirter's before them. But it was far less than sure. And though his imagination fell short of supposing that Sir James was again in active control, he was convinced, from the way that Clements had spoken, that the control of the gang had been taken over by someone who did not recognize Boyle's authority. What would his own position be then? The facts that he had taken orders from Boyle, and that he had been picked up in company with a young woman who was recognized as a police agent and the active enemy of the gang, might of themselves be condoned. They had all taken orders from Boyle till a few hours before. If he were quick enough in his *Le roi est mort: vive le roi*, he might be unblamed for that.

But if Billie should disclose that he had listened while Boyle betrayed all the members and secrets of the gang to the police, that he had used his skill to keep him alive for that purpose, and that he had now been hurrying in her company to get more drugs that he might continue to live, the result for Billie herself might be ill or good—without more knowledge than he had it was hard to say—but for himself, the remaining hours of freedom for those who had been betrayed would be short indeed, if they should be insufficient for the vengeance he had earned.

He did not overlook the fact that, on the other hand, to speak in a way which would imperil his companion's safety had ultimate dangers of a different but serious kind—we have seen already that his wits were sharpened rather than dulled by fear—but the first danger was more deadly, and more acute.

Billie looked at him in a frowning hesitation. She was alert enough to see that he had his own fears, which were different from hers; but she may be excused that she felt her own safety to be the primary consideration for her, and she was in a great doubt as to whether the course which she would have chosen might not be best for both.

There might yet be time to win Clements, either by self-interest or fear—she did not suppose him to be one who would be influenced by more generous motives—to avoid MacWhirter's, to put them down and fly for safety himself, or even to drive them to Bright's Passage, and then back to Rivers Square, with the ultimate object of earning the favour of the police.

She was sure that his name had not appeared on the statement that Boyle had made. If she should tell him that, would he not see the expediency of avoiding a place where the police might already be? But did she want him to avoid it? Might he not turn his course to some other place of which the police knew nothing, where she might be held as hostage or victim? Was it her part, as an agent of Scotland Yard, to turn criminals to avoid the trap?

Inaction is the natural child of doubt, and the next few minutes passed in silence, until they turned down a broad but ill-paved passage, with a warehouse closing its lower end, which had a large white-lettered sign, J. MACWHIRTER & CO. LTD., mounted upon its roof.

CHAPTER XXVI.

BILLIE IS UNFIT TO LIVE

CLEMENTS did not stop the car in the street. He ran into an open gateway, and then turned left-hand into a wide yard that could not be seen from the street, and right-hand into a garage which contained several other cars, executing this manœuvre with a speed and case indicating that he had done it often before.

He jumped out of the car, almost at the second its motion ceased, and opened the rear door for his companions to alight. As he did so, he called to a man who was standing near the gateway: "Bill, you'd better close up now." Bill pushed a heavy sliding gate along its well-oiled groove.

Clements said: "This way, Mr. Webber." His voice was as friendly as ever. He took no notice of Billie at all. What she did, or what Webber might do with her, was to be Webber's concern. It was a matter on which he had had no orders, and on which there was to be no interference from him. Billie observed that he had defined himself very accurately when he said that he took orders, not sides.

Now he led the way to the back of the garage, where a flight of steps rose to a wooden balcony, from which a door opened inwards to a warehouse, piled with great bales of merchandise, and having a musty, spicy scent, faint but penetrating, as though it had been used for such storage for decades, if not centuries, as in fact it had. MacWhirters were Eastern produce merchants of a long-established respectability. Exact in dealings, punctual in payments, having a well-founded reputation for prudent enterprise, few firms and few of the thousand warehouses of the Thames were less likely to arouse the curiosity of the Metropolitan Police.

Webber followed Clements through the warehouse. It may have been a way he already knew. Billie, feeling more hesitation than she allowed to appear, followed Webber, for what else was there to do? She had to abandon the hope that the police would already be on the scene. Well, they might appear at any moment now! Her part must be to act with courage in the meantime.

There was a door at the further end of the warehouse, of which the top half was opaque glass. Clements knocked on it before entering, and as he did so Webber turned back to Billie to whisper hurriedly: "For your life's sake don't talk. Not what Boyle said. Not anything. Leave it to me."

There was no time to reply, nor is it likely that she would have made such a promise. She knew that Webber was not thinking of her. And their interests might not be the same. But the need for caution was plain. His words probably had the effect he wished, so far that they inclined her to wary silence. Let him try first what he could do. The background was a place where she was quite willing to be.

As she thought this, they followed Clements into a room which was plainly but solidly furnished, in a style which asserted the ancient respectability of the firm to which it belonged.

A high desk ran the length of one of the longer walls, with a book rack above it, piled with old ledgers and files. The row of high stools belonged to the period which considered that clerical work could be done more appropriately while seated upon them than with more comfortable chairs at a lower level. Certainly, it would be difficult to go to sleep without falling off.

But Billie had no eyes for the details, though she was aware of the atmosphere of the room. Her glance went first to the man who sat at the head of a table which occupied its central length, and around which three others were gathered. He had the look of a prosperous old-fashioned city merchant, to whom life came easily; who ate and drank much, and slept heavily. His waistcoat rose prominently as he sat, making display of the thick gold watch-chain that crossed it. His face was hard, cruel, in an unimaginative, negative way. One who would be merciless if his safety or his selfish interests were at stake.

Of the others, two were more or less of his own kind; the third, a dryly emaciated man, with a high, narrow, colourless face, appeared to be the clerk which he was. He was filling up cheques in a large cheque-book, writing in the easy flowing hand of a past day. There were other papers scattered upon the table, and the massive door of a tall safe set into the wall was swung open.

There were a row of high, narrow windows along the right-hand side of the room, through which the masts of a lighter showed so closely as to make it evident that the outer wall rose sheer from the bank of the tidal river.

The dawn was broadening now, but three ancient gas-jets over the long desk on the left-hand side of the room were still lighted.

The man at the head of the table looked first at Clements, and at Webber coming in behind him.

"That's right, Clements," he said. "Always trust you to do what's required. We shan't keep you long, Mr. Webber; but there are one or two things that we have to know.... Clements, tell Cale to have the cars ready. We may be going at any moment, and we all want to get back for breakfast. Mr. Shanks is going almost at once."

He spoke in a rich fruity voice, which had a quavering tendency, and Billie noticed that his hand trembled slightly. She judged him to be a nervous man, in bad physical condition.

"Not fit for a bad shock," she thought, "and what a shock he'll get when he knows all that I do now!" She did not guess that there might be much that she did not know, which would have been an unpleasant shock to her.

His eyes were upon her now. "Who is this lady?" he asked. The voice made it clear that strangers were not expected nor welcomed there.

Webber answered. "This is Miss Wingrove. She was with Mr. Boyle. I think she had made some bargain with him. He thought it would be best for her to come with me."

There was little in this statement to which Billie could object, and nothing that was not true, though it left much to be said.

MacWhirter's eyes had a look of puzzled astonishment as he answered: "Oh, *Miss Wingrove*? Yes, Miss Wingrove, of course. Read" (turning to the clerk at his left hand), "I think you'd better take her into.... No, let her stay here. It can make no difference now.... Miss Wingrove, you can take the chair by the window.... Mr. Webber, there's a chair there. Pull it up to the table.... What we want to know is what's happened to Mr. Boyle. How he is now. And if there's been any traffic about it with the police. Just the facts. Nothing more."

Webber still kept to the narrow path of truth, though he used it sparely. "Mr. Boyle's been poisoned. I've saved his life, so far. I was on the way back to my office to get another injection for him when Clements picked me up. If I'm not very quick about it, he will certainly die. He may be dead now."

"Very sad. Very sad. But there may still be more urgent matters. What about the police?"

"I can tell you this. There is an Inspector Cauldron—a C.I.D. man—at Boyle's flat. He's just sitting watching. I don't know how he comes to be there."

143

A voice which Billie did not like interposed from one of the other men at the table. "I expect Miss Wingrove could tell us that."

She found all eyes turned upon her. Hostile all, except Webber's, in which dread of what she might be going to say was more easy to read. "He may have come to see that I was all right," she replied casually. Webber should have every chance to put matters right for her in his own way. And, meanwhile, the minutes passed. Surely Superintendent Backwash would have done something by now?

"And," the same man said sharply, "he may have followed you here?"

"Well, why not?" she echoed. Surely there could be no harm in them thinking that!

"Certainly not," MacWhirter said, as though an unseemly possibility had been proposed. "You can trust Clements not to have overlooked that.... Mr. Webber, is there anything else which we ought to know?"

"No. I don't think there is."

"Then I don't think we need detain you longer. We are much obliged for what you have done. But it will not be necessary for you to make any further efforts to save Mr. Boyle's life. He appears to have come under suspicion of the police, and therefore become a danger to us. A gentleman whose name need not be mentioned has taken over control. His orders are for operations of all kinds to be suspended immediately, and for traces of recent activities to be covered up. But that will not directly affect you. Absolute silence will be your safe-guard, as it will be ours. Universally exercised, it is an invincible shield. In a few minutes, I will arrange for you to be taken wherever you want to go.... You have a mission of life-saving in which you should not appear negligent, however regrettably futile it is to be....

"Miss Wingrove, you are a sensible young woman. You have sense enough to know when a game is lost, and not to make a fuss which can be of no advantage to you.

"From whatever motives, you have interfered with matters in which you have no concern. You have caused more trouble than we have experienced from any other direction either here or in other countries. You have jeopardized business interests of great magnitude. It is hardly too much to say that you have been responsible for the deaths of two men—I allude to Cornelius Mildew and Peter Boyle, who is dying now—of more importance than you could ever expect to be. It is an activity which obviously cannot be allowed to continue. Your activities have gone far to produce a position in which none of us would be safe."

He paused and looked round the table as he said this, and received an assenting murmur which was actually a sentence of death—and such a one as was to be executed with far greater celerity than is the custom of official justice.

He went on: "You will be wise in your own interest if you take the position quietly. You have no possible means of escape. If you are reasonable you will be dealt with in the quietest and speediest manner, and it will be over in—well, almost at once."

It would be wrong to say that Billie listened to this obituary counsel with an undisturbed mind. She knew that she was in critical peril, though she had no more than a vague idea of what their next procedure would be likely to be. She knew, of course, that the heroes and heroines of fiction are never executed by their lawless enemies until they have been tied up for a sufficient period to allow reasonable opportunities of being rescued or wriggling free. But she had no confidence that this curious procedure would be followed. It seemed unlikely that it would appeal to the prudence of business men.

Yet she had some confidence in a position on which she thought, with partial truth, that she was much better informed than they.

She said boldly: "Before you get more into the soup than you are now, you might get Mr. Webber to tell what really happened."

Webber saw his dilemma. Should he fail to support her now, he could have little hope of after-mercy from the police. But that was if they should come to know. Boyle dead—Billie dead—what could be safer for him than that? And there was a nearer deadlier danger—deadlier than the police would ever be likely to be—that was round him now.

"I don't know what she's talking about," he replied, "but you can be sure she's trying to gain time with a clever lie. She has one of the most unscrupulous tongues that I ever heard. She's only playing for time. If you begin listening—"

"Miss Wingrove," MacWhirter said, "it's no use trying that game with us. We've heard too much about you already. And we've no time. If it were otherwise, I should be glad for you to talk. I've no doubt you could tell us things that we should like to know. But now we've no time at all.... Read, tell Clements I want him here."

Billie saw that time was becoming short. The physical odds against her were already hopelessly bad, and would become worse. The police did not come. It was time to play any trumps she had.

"When I tell you," she said, "that Mr. Boyle has signed a full confession, and that Sir James Shorter was arrested a few hours ago, perhaps you'll understand that it's not I who am in any danger.... Mr. MacWhirter," she concluded, looking into the eyes of the man who she thought to be the most cowardly there, "when your times comes, what a rope you'll need!"

The remark would have been tactless at any time. It might be considered particularly inopportune now, but her object had not been to conciliate, but to terrify, if she could. She saw that her words had not been without effect, but the man for whom they were most directly intended appeared to be least impressed.

"Miss Wingrove," he said, "I've told you that you do no good for yourself by these reckless lies. Do you really ask me to believe that Sir—the gentleman you mentioned—is under arrest?"

"Yes. He was arrested last night. He's at Scotland Yard now."

Mr. MacWhirter looked round the table. "Gentlemen," he said, "I can tell you, from my own certain knowledge, that that is a lie. He was issuing orders from his own house less than four hours ago. But you will agree with me that this young woman knows too much for it to be healthy for us. Read, I must have Clements at once."

The clerk, who had stood in some hesitation while this conversation concluded, now turned to execute his errand. He stepped to the wall, and whistled down a speaking-tube, raising the earpiece to listen for the reply.

He appeared to be listening for some time, so that MacWhirter broke out impatiently: "Well, don't be all day! Isn't Clements there? Get Cale or someone. Go down, if you can't get any reply."

Read spoke now, in a shaking voice: "It's Inspector Cauldron, sir. He wants an assurance that Miss Wingrove is safe. He says he's prepared to shoot you up, if necessary, but he doesn't want her to get in any danger."

MacWhirter was breathing heavily. His words seemed to come with difficulty. "Where's he speaking from now?"

"He's in the garage. He says it's no use resisting. The police are all round the place."

"Tell him," MacWhirter said feebly, "that we don't resist the police. It isn't the kind of thing there could be any occasion to do. Of course, Miss Wingrove's quite safe. He might have known she'd be safe with us.... You mustn't take anything I said seriously, Miss Wingrove. You've got a sense of humour, I hope. I've been worried, you know. I've been worried from every side."

"Yes, I've got a sense of humour all right," Billie answered, with a sudden uncontrollable laugh at the removal of all her fears.

"But you'll need it more than I.... It does seem absurd to think of how you were threatening me a moment ago."

Read was speaking again: "Inspector Cauldron says will Miss Wingrove go down to the garage. She's to go alone, and everyone else is to stay here."

Billie lost no time in complying with this request. She said, "So long, Mr. Webber. Thanks for all the help you've been," as she passed that gentleman, to his obvious discomfiture, but she was gone before he could think of any useful reply.

CHAPTER XXVII.

MAINLY CONCERNING ROPES

INSPECTOR CAULDRON said: "You see, Humphries' gun has come in useful at last."

Billie answered: "At last! I like that. Don't you think I found it useful to me?"

They were looking at Clements and three other men lined up against the garage wall.

"Well, I want you to keep them covered while I fetch help from outside. I shan't be more than three minutes."

"You mean you're alone?"

"Yes. Boyle's dead. So I'd nothing better to do."

"Why hasn't Superintendent Backwash sent anyone here?"

"Because Sir Henry Bracken came back—and he released Shorter—and—in fact, there's been an infernal muddle—but we mustn't talk now."

"I'd rather fetch the help, if you don't mind. If I keep pointing it at them, I shall shoot one of them, more likely than not."

"Very well. They're not formidable. Just rats. But I don't want them to run."

"Mr. Clements—that's the one at the end—won't be any trouble if you talk to him in the right voice. He takes orders, not sides. He was just going to have an order to murder me."

"Billie, you're a bit excited. Please do what I ask at once. Go to the call-box at the end of the passage, and ask the Wren Street station to send enough men here to remove—how many are there upstairs?"

"Five."

"To remove nine men. We'll think out what the charges are when we've got them there. I'm glad that I'm here in time."

"Cyril, you were a dear. I don't mind telling you I thought you would never come."

With these words she at last made for the door, but found that there would be no occasion to go further than that. A police car, from which a uniformed squad were descending, stood in the yard.

Superintendent Backwash was in advance. He looked at her with obvious relief. "I'm glad," he said, "that you've come to no harm."

"Yes," she answered, "but you've got Inspector Cauldron to thank for that."

"I don't care who I thank," the superintendent replied.

"But there's one thing for which we've all got to thank you. Today's going to make an end of the Mildew Gang."

"I told Mr. MacWhirter," she replied, "that he would need an extra thick rope. He didn't seem to like the idea."

"I don't know about MacWhirter. I'm not sure how much we shall be able to bring home to him. Sir James Shorter certainly will.... But we mustn't stand talking now."

ABOUT THE AUTHOR

SYDNEY FOWLER WRIGHT (1874-1965) penned over seventy volumes of science fiction, fantasy, classic mysteries, historical novels, poetry, and non-fiction, many of them being published by the Borgo Press Imprint of Wildside Press.